RUTHIE PINCUS OF BROOKLYN

Helena Clare Pittman

Two Paths Press

Other books by Helena Clare Pittman

A Grain of Rice	*Martha and the Nightbird*
The Gift of the Willows	*Counting Jennie*
Once When I Was Scared	*Miss Hindy's Cats*
Gerald-Not-Practical	*Where Will You Swim Tonight?*
One Quiet Morning	*Uncle Phil's Diner*
Still Life Stew	*Sunrise*
The Snowman's Path	*Crow Flies*
A Dinosaur for Gerald	*The Angel Tree*

First printing 2012
Second printing March 2013
Third printing July 2013
Forth printing November 2014

Printed in the United States of America

ISBN 978-0-615-69983-7

ACKNOWLEDGMENTS

Since publishing began its huge corporate and then electronic shift that resulted in the loss of this book's editors, my friends and work partners became my editors and writing coaches in their stead. I am so grateful to my friend, Jillian Higgins, who kept me swimming when I couldn't see the book's other shore. And to Louise Lumen, who, it happens to be my dumb luck, loves listening to me read these chapters to her. My thanks also go to the writers groups, peers and students, who suffered through the book's years of revisions. And to Diane Arico, who was my editor at Dial Books For Young Readers, who wanted to publish this work but was prevented by the trends of the book market, thank you for loving Ruthie into life.

Thanks, too, to Debby Vetter, and Marianne Carus, my editor and editor in chief at *Cricket* Magazine, for so much acceptance and patronage of my work over more than twenty years, and for publishing parts of this writing: "Rose Petals," "Midnight Green" and "Circles in the Sand." Thanks to Emily Kelley, my editor for nearly ten years at Carolrhoda Books, Lerner Publications, for publishing "Uncle Phil's Diner," another story with Ruthie Pincus and her father that became part of the Smithsonian List in 1998.

Particular thanks go to my agent, Edythea Ginis Selman, for her support of my work over these twenty-five years, and for her friendship; a person whose praises no psalm can adequately sing.

Part of the life of this work is owed to author Johanna Hurwitz, who mentored me with this writing in the course of my Masters of Arts work. Thank you, too, to the editors who considered this work, and gave me invaluable editorial input and support during publishing hard times and transitions.

This expression of thanks would be incomplete without the acknowledgement of my dear friend and publisher at Maple Hill Press, Julie Fleck, who listened to this work for so many years, offering her wise counsel and later, to her son, Chris Fleck, for his beautiful design of the cover and pages, and his guidance through the process of publishing the Author's Edition of this book.

And to my son, Galen, for coming with me to Crown Street to photograph and paint number 657 for the cover illustration of this book. I imagine his grandparents, his Aunt Jo, Aunt Rose, his great grandparents and all the family, smiling, sitting on the green metal chairs on the porch, understanding the wonder of it all.

PREFACE

The story of Ruthie Pincus grew out of my root memories of childhood on Crown Street. The family that slowly took shape through my writing differed from my own. I had one sibling, my older sister, Jolene. But in any life there is one story above the surface and another below. The character of Ruthie's older brother, Leon, certainly grew out of my yearning. But characters that rise up inside are a mystery. They express things that press to have life and fullness, to embody needs that are deep and need to find fulfillment. At any rate, all the characters in this writing came forward and took what was my childhood and made it full, made it a place to which I was and still am drawn in some consoling and healing way.

The mental illness of my dearly loved Aunt Rose, and her death from a prefrontal lobotomy, the only "cure" available in the 1950s for her depressive illness, for that's what I've come to think she suffered from, caused unknown depths of agonies to my family, for it was unshared. But the need in me to assemble a narrative of its role in my parents' lives and behavior, and its impact on me, was clearly pressing, and surprised me when it surfaced.

At the same time, the unfolding news from Europe, of the Nazi madness, was the air we children unknowingly breathed. Too much evil to speak to us of, or perhaps to speak of at all. I can only imagine the self-protective denial, as well as the agony and terror suffered by the adults around me. My grandparents emigrated here in 1901, fleeing the Russian persecutions of the Jews — the pogroms. But after World War II, letters that had for years crossed back and forth over the oceans between my family and the family they left behind in Russia, stopped. What terrors of my own were born in the terrible silence? I will never know, yet writing about this family has added to my life more than I could have imagined possible.

Yet humor was central to my family, beginning with my wonderful father and flourishing in my sister, and in me. But I lost my parents early, and within five years, the rest of my parents' generation passed away. Our close-knit family, clustered mostly in Crown Heights, Brooklyn, moved apart, opening a painful emptiness in me. Twenty years later, with the loss of my sister, I stood alone, and the character of Ruthie Pincus came into being. In "Ruthie..." the world I was born into lives again — a family and extended family of neighbors, their sufferings and their laughter — and I am there with them.

DEDICATION

All this I have inherited from
my grandmother, Anna Bailenson.

To Aunt Rose,
and for my mother, as promised.

CONTENTS

BOOK ONE

BOOK TWO

BOOK THREE

BOOK FOUR

BOOK FIVE

BOOK ONE

Crown Street

The sun is warm on my skin
My doll carriage is khaki green
Made of oil cloth.
My doll, Hannah, is lying inside, covered with a flannel blanket.

I feel my hair, fine, the breeze ruffling it,
See the concrete squares passing under my feet,
My small, red, buckled, wing-tipped sandals, patinaed with shoe polish.
I love the faces on these shoes,
Miniatures of my mother's brown ones.

Vibrating through my hands,
The sidewalk's cast edges,
Its bumps and pebbles
Rattle the carriage's white-painted metal, hard,
    rubber-rimmed wheels.

I smell the wool sweater I'm wearing, buttoned to my neck,
And know my mother knitted it.

The neighborhood afternoon murmurs around me,
Children and adult voices.
Wheeling Hannah
To the shadow line
Where the tall maples start,
Where I turn back,
Warm in that sunshine,
Breathing the breeze moving my hair in slow motion,
Hannah's carriage wheels squeaking,

I'm stepping my way down Crown Street.

A Tree In The Holy Land

My grandmother and I play cards.
Our game is Casino.
I learn to add numbers.
She tells me stories
About my grandfather,
About the way they left Lithuanian Russia
Where they lived in danger.

This is a photograph
Taken with my eyes
And something deeper than eyes
But hidden,
Deeper than cameras in my flesh
Maybe even outside of me
Where my shadow follows over the concrete streets of Brooklyn
Swimming along the parked cars.

My grandfather had a printing press concealed in the floor.

Cossacks, soldiers, one day came to my grandparents' house to
    find it.

A picture of a man hung on the wall.
Something about him caused them to ask who he was.

My grandmother told them it was her uncle.
But it was Karl Marx.

The soldiers searched but found nothing.
They left and so did my grandparents.

My grandmother sailed to America.
My grandfather hid, like the undiscovered printing press.
He saved money to follow my grandmother.

When my grandmother told this to me
The air changed.

I saw in her blue eyes that there was more to this story.
That she knew I was too young to bear its burden.

Her silence moved into the ground of me
Where, in time, it grew into an understanding:
Beside the family I knew
There were people who were before me that are also my family.
They swam beside me like the shadows on the cars parked
    along Crown Street.

Their stories are my history,

And my mother's and father's, my sister's and my brothers',
My cousins' and aunts' and uncles',
And everyone's' whom we knew in our neighborhood in Brooklyn.

We were all part of it,
And of each other.

Once when we played Casino
My grandmother told me she had wanted to go to Palestine,
To the Promised Land.

In that picture my grandmother's eyes shine with tears.

Palestine, she said.
And her eyes are the thing I can't forget.

Then she told me there was a tree planted there
With my name on it.

One night
Long after my grandmother died,

And my grandfather,
And my mother and father,

I dreamed of Mamma.

Write about Rose,
Rose—

Write about her! She said.

And in the dream I understood.
I will! I promised.

But as I came out of sleep
My understanding faded with the dream.
Who was Rose?

But I know now the dream could only have meant one person.
Mamma's sister, Aunt Rose,
Who glowed, like my grandmother's eyes when she told me the story
    of the printing press.

Aunt Rose's laughter was like the sunshine.
And she shone with things that couldn't be said out loud.

Yet it seems someone heard them,
Me.
And the pictures I took
I saved
Until I could look carefully at them,
To tell their stories.

Maybe my grandfather's printing press is still buried
    in the dirt in Vilna.

And somewhere in Palestine
There's a tree.

Tall and thick and beautiful by now.
There are letters in the earth that read:
Ruthie Pincus.

Mamma, Pappa, Leon, Rebecca and Georgie

Sometimes my mother asks me, or my older sister, Rebecca, to wash the dishes. Sometimes Leon, my older brother, takes a turn. So does Georgie, my younger brother.

Georgie has to stand on a chair to reach the sink. Mamma doesn't allow Georgie to wash the actual dishes because they're glass, but saves him the pots and pans. She then has to wash these again. Sometimes she just gives him pots and pans that are already clean, just to teach Georgie responsibility. Then Georgie likes to wear Mamma's yellow rubber gloves which are entirely too big for him, and which he sometimes fills with water instead of washing the pots and pans. Mamma intervenes then, and reminds Georgie that the pots and pans need to be clean so that she can use them to cook our food. Then Georgie asks if he can take her gloves, filled with water, out to the porch and drop them over the concrete railing, just once. Mamma says no, pretty firmly, and again tells Georgie how much she and his family need him to wash the pots and pans. Learning responsibility, Georgie begins scrubbing a pot, lathering the soap into bubbles. Georgie has discovered that he can launch these bubbles across the kitchen, and sometimes even as far as the dinette. Mamma tries to be patient with Georgie but sometimes she's just too tired.

Most often my mother washes the dishes herself. This is the time she sings and talks to God.

My mother doesn't usually say the things she

5

thinks—at least not in the course of ordinary life. Her mouth pinches up instead. But my mother's dish-washing life is another matter. When Mamma washes dishes she sings opera. She sways and sings a kind of soprano gibberish—a kind of Italian, or French. This is when my mother expresses the things that are behind her frowns, her pursed lips, her sighs. Mamma's beautiful voice rises, hits high notes that reach out the open window in summer, drifting over Crown Street, foreign-sounding and operatic, like the radio. Music runs in our family. But it isn't long before Mamma shifts to English and the spoken word and asks God to deliver her, from Rebecca and me fighting, or Georgie's temper tantrums, or her worry about money. Then she slips into Yiddish, her voice pleading. And I lose track of my mother's worries.

When the dishes are done so is my mother's prayer time. She becomes herself again, frowning and worried about what the neighbors think of Georgie's screaming. But if you want to know something about what my mother is thinking you have to wait until she does the dishes.

My father also knows more than he says. I see it by his forehead when it furrows. Pappa's sighs are louder than Mamma's. And they end with his voice—an intake of breath then a kind of eee-yahhh! But in the morning Pappa whistles, cooking oatmeal, squeezing fresh oranges for juice. The orange fragrance travels down the hall and finds me in my room, my first awareness of the day sometimes mixed with my dreams. And when I join him in the kitchen the bubbling oatmeal seems to express Pappa's morning cheer. He stands at the stove stirring the pot, a towel draped over his head after his shower. Pappa is losing his hair. He doesn't want to catch a chill and get sick. Shuffling from the stove to the table in his moccasins, his green eyes twinkle as he greets me. With the towel over his head it looks as if he is saying some kind of prayer too.

My older sister, Rebecca, wore braces until last year. And she had pimples. Her neck seemed too long. Then her braces came off, her pimples disappeared, and her long neck looked suddenly beautiful. And she met Sam. Rebecca calls me stupid, though it upsets our parents, and, of course, me. It's one of the things my mother talks to God about when she washes dishes. But there are also times I think Rebecca loves me more than she loves anyone else in the world. It just depends on her mood. And since Sam she has become much nicer.

Leon is my older brother. He spends his time studying, working at Finder's Grocery and practicing football. But now and then he stops at my door, on his way from the bathroom to his room, and asks me what I'm doing, and we talk and smile. When Leon is making a delivery for Finder's and sees me on the street he calls out to me. "Ruthie!" comes Leon's voice suddenly into my playing, and I can't stop my feet from running toward him. And if I'm on skates I hold on to the back of his bike and he pulls me along, the wind making ripples in his blond hair, my wild pony tail sailing straight out behind us.

My little brother Georgie is two. Sometimes he's cranky—well more than sometimes. Life is organized around Georgie's naps and bedtime. Everyone has to whisper when he's sleeping. Georgie, we've figured out, is temperamental. Sometimes he just cries until he falls asleep. Nobody can make him stop. Not by holding him, or calling him "Bubela", which means "baby" in Yiddish, or by telling him how much they love him. He just cries until he's exhausted, and so are we. Then the house is quiet except that Georgie snores and Rebecca complains that she can't concentrate on her homework. "Are you kidding?" asks our brother, Leon. "Georgie's snores are like music! Music!" Leon repeats. "Music! M-eeuuww-siccc!"

Though I'd like to roll my eyes when Leon says this, I smile at the way his eyes go wide and at the way his voice is rising high, and I'm thinking, music really does run in our family. "Meewwwww-siccccc!" says Leon, and I see Pappa's head turn. I see the look that passes between my parents. I see my father's mouth twitch, and I start laughing and I have to admit Leon looks a little wild. Then our mother takes Leon by the arm and sometimes shakes him, saying, "Shah!" nearly frantic that Leon's voice and Pappa's and my laughter will wake Georgie. And when we calm down, and the sound of Georgie's snoring buzzes through the hallway, Mamma sighs. Pappa sighs with that sound his voice makes. The house is filled with our sighs, of relief and frustration, Georgie's snores sounding like an airplane making lazy circles in and out of white, puffy clouds and blue sky on a summer's day.

That is often the time when Mamma washes dishes or the kitchen cabinets and counters, singing opera, in her odd French and Italian, asking God what she's done to deserve all this, while the water in the kitchen runs along like a Cantor singing at a Synagogue, and the glass dishes that once belonged to Pappa's mother and father—the grandparents who died before I was born—get washed, and the kitchen gets scrubbed clean.

Me, I'm Ruthie Pincus, almost ten.

Finder's

Mamma won't be home. I remember on the way up Troy Avenue after school. She and Aunt Loolie are shopping. I check for the key hanging on the ribbon under my sweater, warm, pressed against my skin. I look back toward the schoolyard. No sign of Aylene Muntzer. I touch Mamma's shopping list folded in my jumper pocket, ingredients for soup written in her big pencil letters on the small rectangle of yellow paper my father brings home from night school.

"Ruthie Pincus!" Mr. Finder greets me from behind a tower of wooden food crates. "Shopping for your Mamma?" I wave the list. I enter the store. It smells of pickled herring and bread and the sawdust on the wooden floor. Finder's Grocery is dark after the street.

"Vait, vait, vait..." says a voice from the ceiling. Mrs. Finder is scowling down at me from a tall, wooden ladder, leaning against a shelf of boxes and cans. The floor shakes as, rung by rung, she lowers her bulk. "Yeh?" she asks, squinting at me with her small, brown, sharp eyes, looking as if they are set a little too closely together. Her light brown, gray-streaked hair is tightly braided, wrapped around the back of her head like a halo. A pair of glasses hangs from a dark grosgrain ribbon, its ends knotted around the handles of the glasses, resting on her big chest covered in her starched apron. Mrs. Finder is wearing a pencil behind her ear.

I hold out my mother's list. Mrs. Finder lifts her glasses and puts them on. "One pound onions," she reads and looks at me. Brown eyes lock into mine. "Your

9

Mamma is making soup?" I nod. Mrs. Finder walks to the vegetable shelves. She fills a paper bag with onions. She straightens, purses her lips as if to receive a kiss and sets the bag on a shelf. She looks over at me again. "Parsley," she says. Again I nod. "Parsley, parsley," she repeats, separating out a bunch, shaking it from a larger clump. She snaps open a small brown paper bag from a pile on the shelf, puts the parsley inside and folds the bag closed. Then she looks back to the list. "Three parsnips, noodles, celery—a seeded rye bread, sliced." Frowning, she finds the parsnips and celery. "Noodles, noodles," she's now calling softly, scanning the shelves until her eyes spot the noodle boxes in a corner, at the very top.

Next to the ladder leans a long wooden pole with a metal grip. Mrs. Finder groans as she drags the ladder to the corner. She grasps the grip at the same time.

"Can I help?" I ask, thinking I could lift one side of the ladder, maybe hold the grip for her. I'm longing to feel it in my hands, try it out, see what it's like to hook a box of noodles and let it fall from the top shelf, then catch it like a football, the way my brother, Leon, does when he's working at Finder's. "We're going for the touchdown!" I can hear Leon say.

But Leon is at football practice, and only Mrs. Finder is here now. She looks down at me. "Vait—," she grunts, the ladder and gripper scraping along the floor, making three trails in the sawdust. I move toward her. She waves me away, sets the gripper down, wriggles the ladder, settles it against the high, corner shelf. Then she pulls herself up one, two, three, four, five rungs as I watch. "Hold it!" she says. "The gripper pole?" I ask. She looks down at me and frowns. "The ladder..." she answers. "Okay," she says next, pointing to the gripper. I pick it up and hand it up to her. She takes it, squeezes its handle.

The metal fingers close around a noodle box, raising a cloud of dust. Mrs. Finder lets the pole slide through her hand until the box is pointing at me. She lets the box drop. I catch it, feeling the beat of my heart. Mrs. Finder lowers herself to the floor, takes the box from my hands, dusts it with her apron and gives it back. "Soup, soup, soup, soo-p!" she sings the words in a little melody, turning back to the list as if nothing has happened. As if using that gripper pole was as common as the sawdust.

I am looking with admiration at Mrs. Finder when suddenly she declares, "Tomatoes!" and looks at me. "Vy didn't you tell me before?" I open my mouth to tell her I didn't know. I want to say it was written that way on my mother's list. But I just look at Mrs. Finder and watch her lips purse as she turns. I follow her back to the vegetable shelves as one by one she examines the tomatoes. "One penny each," she's saying, choosing one with a black spot and one that's got a soft, deep, red dent. "Good for soup!"

Now Mrs. Finder pulls off her glasses. They fall against the big cushion of her chest—big as two mountains. Looking up at her they almost block out the slow, whirring ceiling fan, like mountains block the moon. She moves behind the counter and selects a rye bread from its shelf, places it on the polished metal slicing machine, touches the switch. The motor rumbles. The store trembles, jars clinking together, as sharp iron prongs close over the bread, cutting a row of slices. Suddenly the air is filled with the fragrance of fresh rye and caraway seeds.

When the ingredients for my mother's soup sit on the wooden counter, Mrs. Finder pulls out a large brown bag, snaps it open, and takes the pencil from behind her ear. While she scribbles numbers onto the bag my eyes wander to a jar of wrapped candies next to the cash register. I count three in gold and blue foil—hazelnut and milk chocolate. One is sitting at the very top of the jar, just under its lid. My mouth waters. When I get my allowance, Monday, I'm thinking, I'll come back.

Then I feel Mrs. Finder looking at me. I turn and our eyes lock again. Then she glances at the jar of candy, her mouth puckered. "A dollar-thirty-three cents," she tells me. I hold out Mamma's two dollars. Frowning, Mrs. Finder opens and smooths them on the counter. She hits a key on the cash register. "Sixty-seven cents change!" she calls over the clang of the register bell hanging in the air. Then she looks at me. "Thank you," I tell her, taking the change. I pick up the package and turn to go. "Ruthie Pincus!" she says startling me. "Yes?" I turn back. Mrs. Finder lifts the cover of the jar. She takes the foil wrapped hazelnut chocolate and holds it out to me. Though Mrs. Finder's face doesn't seem made for smiling, her mouth turns up and the frown above her nose becomes a row of red vertical lines.

"Oh!" I say, I open my mouth to thank her, reaching, accepting the candy from her. Suddenly, past Mrs. Finder's ear, Aylene Muntzer is on the other side of the big, front window, walking with Joannie Nevins. "Uh—thanks—uh—Mrs.—uh—" I'm holding the candy in one hand while feeling for the shape of my key through my sweater with the other. Then my thoughts start racing: "Mamma-won't-be-home-until-four-thirty..." Now I'm holding on to Mrs. Finder by her eyes. "Uh—Mrs. Finder..." I say, watching as furrows form around the red lines over her nose again. "I could—uh—stay—and help, I'd like that—you don't have to pay me—I could climb up on the ladder and straighten the shelves—I could dust them, uh, get things down you may need with the gripper pole—" I'm talking as fast as the words will come out of my mouth.

In slow motion Mrs. Finder's gaze has moved beyond me in the direction of her husband. "Yussel!" she's calling to Mr. Finder. "We need more pot cheese the shelf is empty! Yussel!"

Mrs. Finder turns back to me. Aylene turns at the same time. Aylene's and my eyes lock. My stomach sinks like an elevator. Mr. Finder, approaches, smiles, tries to pass me but my legs won't move. Holding the brown bag of groceries I watch Aylene and Joannie through the window, making their way up Troy Avenue. Now Joannie Nevins looks over her shoulder, smiles in my direction, whispers something to Aylene. I look up at Mr. Finder. Mr. Finder looks down at me. He's waiting for me to leave, to speak, to do something. My mouth is open. I'm looking at him and at Aylene and Joannie, walking down the street over his shoulder. Mr. Finder's smile begins to droop. Joannie and Aylene disappear behind the window molding. "The pot cheese! Pot cheeeese!" Mrs. Finder is calling. Her lips are pursed. Her eyes look beady, the furrows look like pillows. She isn't looking at me anymore. It's as if I am not there, as if I hadn't asked her anything. As if she was someone else now, not the person who had given me the hazelnut candy pressed in the fist of my hand, sweaty and soft.

"Yes—coming!" Mr. Finder answers her.

Aylene Muntzer

I start up Troy Avenue, walking as slowly as I can, hoping Aylene and Joannie will be gone by the time I round the corner onto Crown Street. I count the shells in the concrete of the sidewalk. I count the squares, the hand prints, the shoe prints, the number of GGs Georgie Goldstein's fingers drew when the cement was wet. I look at the sky, noticing how clear it is, how blue. Wanting to stop and just look at that blue, blue sky, wanting to fill my lungs with the clear, cool air. But my feet keep moving. Then I'm at the corner, then I'm rounding the curve of hedges growing against Joannie Nevins' apartment house. And then I'm seeing Joannie leaning against the door, and Aylene facing her, except for her green eyes which are looking at me.

Then she is turning to Joannie. "I have to do homework..." Aylene tells Joannie.

"Me too," Joannie is answering, pushing herself against the big iron and glass door. "Guess I'll see you tomorrow," says Joannie. "Hey, Joannie?" says Aylene, but Joannie has already disappeared inside the building. Aylene looks blankly at the door. Then she turns to look at me again. Her green eyes flash before she starts up Crown Street.

I walk two houses behind, as slowly as I can to still be walking, waiting for Aylene to reach the middle of the block where the maple trees grow thick and shadowy, dividing Aylene's Crown Street from mine. She's walking slowly too. Aylene's shoes have taps. I can hear their metal strike the concrete as she walks. She stops in front of the Berman's house. She opens her school bag, rummages around, looking for something. Then she looks at me. Snake greens glitter through my head. My feet keep moving. The distance closes between us.

Aylene Muntzer has two voices, one when other people are around and one when Aylene and I are alone. It's the second one that comes out of her mouth now. She doesn't say, "Hello, Ruthie." No. She doesn't say, "you're walking slowly and so am I. Walking as slowly as the film in your father's movie projector when the light starts to flicker and the film begins to come off the reel in a slow, helpless tangle, and everyone's hands and feet and smiles look like they're under water and their voices would be moaning if we could hear them. Like everyone who is supposed to be enjoying themselves is pushing against a wall of time, as if thcy would like to move faster so that they can look like themselves again, so their voices can have laughter in them again, but all they can do is move more and more and more slowly. And they can't stop if they want to, and your father is trying to untangle the film, asking *what the heck's the matter with this thing?* as he pulls off his glasses to get a closer look, to see it in the dark, saying, Miriam, turn on that darn light, will you? And he isn't really saying heck or darn."

No, Aylene doesn't say that. Instead she asks, "Ruthie, do you have your math workbook?" And I just keep walking toward her in the same slow motion as the film in my father's projector.

Aylene gets bigger and bigger, begins to look wavy through the wall of water that sits on my eyes. I imagine turning, hurrying back to Troy Avenue to the corner, and the big apartment house on Montgomery Street where my aunt is minding Georgie. Instead I hear myself answer. "I need it to do my homework, Aylene!" My voice comes out so loud I jump. Aylene jumps too.

My walk has changed. My shoes have no taps but I hear my heels strike the pavement, just their leather. I hear them as I brush past Aylene. Hear the soles scrape as I climb the fourteen concrete steps to my door. I ring the bell even though I know there's no one upstairs to hear it. I jiggle the latch, killing time, one hand burrowing under my clothes, feeling for the key but there's nothing hanging from the ribbon. I feel my skin sticky. My hand travels to the elastic band of my skirt, and the key is there. It slips into my underpants as I try to grab it.

I look over my shoulder. Aylene's snake eyes are glowing up at me like a special effect. "She's in the shower—my mother's in the shower," I say, but Aylene's figured it out, figured out that we're really alone and when we're alone Aylene wants to fight. That's the way Aylene is. Donna Pukatch likes to ride horses. I like to collect stamps, and rocks and plastic charms. Aylene Muntzer likes to fight. With me. "She'll be out in three minutes, she takes fast showers!"

Aylene starts up the steps. I hear her metal toe taps. I hold my breath. Then we're both distracted. A wheel that needs to be greased is singing. My mother wheeling Georgie in the stroller, I'm thinking, what a relief! But it's Mrs. Greene, walking the twins.

"Hi, Mrs. Greene!" I call, trying to stop her with my voice, "how are your daughters?" forcing out my words like hands that would close around the shiny chrome of the twins' stroller. "Hello, girls," answers Mrs. Greene smiling. "They're fine thank you, Ruthie. How nice of you to ask!" Then Mrs. Greene is four houses away in the maple gloom.

While Aylene is turned in her direction I put my hand down my sweater, under the elastic waistband of my underpants, grope for the key which is ready to burrow its way through a leg elastic, grab it, pull it up through the neck of my sweater and stab the lock. But the door pushes open before I can turn it. "Is that you, Ruthie?" calls my mother from upstairs. "How are you, Aylene?" My mother is rubbing her hair with a towel. I look up the stairs with an open mouth then down the stoop to Aylene, whose mouth is open too. "We got home a little early," says my mother. "I was in the shower. There was no hot water this morning. The boiler was broken." Now I dimly remember brushing my teeth and washing before school, cold water coming out of the hot water tap. Then I hear Georgie

16

start screaming. "Did you stop at Finder's?" My mother asks. "Be right there, Georgie!" she calls, and disappears from the upstairs doorway. "Uh huh," I whisper. I step through the door then turn to face Aylene. Only then do I feel the hazelnut chocolate, soft and slimy, oozing through its wrapper in my fist.

"Well, can I borrow it?" she's asking. But her voice has already begun its change back to normal—if normal has anything to do with Aylene. I picture Mrs. Muntzer who chased Donna Pukatch and me when we rode our bikes past Aylene's, and Donna's bike hit a hole in the sidewalk and Donna fell and skinned her elbow and bright red patches of blood appeared like oddly shaped roses on her white blouse. Though Aylene is speaking softly now it's that voice I hear, high pitched and screaming. "Well can I borrow it?" she's asking.

"I already told you," I answer. "I need it to do my homework." My hand, the one without the chocolate, is closing on the doorknob.

I look down the stoop at Aylene, her foot still on the first step. "I left mine at school," Aylene says quietly. I catch a glint of rattlesnake green as the door scrapes shut.

I climb the stairs slowly, licking the sweet, gooey hazelnut chocolate.

Pictures

I'm drawing pictures at the dining room table. My grandmother is crocheting. "Mamela, a game of cards?" she asks. "He's reading his *Forvitz*, your grandpa."

She's mixing Yiddish and English, tilting her head toward the archway that leads to the living room.

"It's a shame, a shanda!" murmurs my grandfather. He rattles the pages of *The Forward*, The Jewish

17

newspaper he writes for.

He's highly educated, my mother tells us with pride.

Under the reading lamp my grandfather's features cast sharp shadows, darkening one side of his face.

Aristocratic! Mamma and her sisters like to say of him. They resemble my grandfather, chiseled noses and high cheekbones. But my grandfather's eyes smolder with intensity.

Unlike my grandmother, Grandpa Sam speaks perfect English. His voice is rich, like the music he loves, Beethoven and Brahms, music his daughter, my Aunt Rose plays on the piano.

"Vultures!" he says now, under his breath. "Vultures and parasites—in America!" He turns the page, slapping the paper to straighten it. The sound drowns out his next words. But I can hear his voice, dark, in a minor key.

"In America your grandchildren can walk down the street," my grandmother answers. Her words hang in the air.

Spiel

My sister Rebecca's nose is fine like my grandfather's. Mine is short like the Pincuses, Pappa's family. Rebecca says it looks like a pancake. She says I have a pudding face.

"Pudding Face!" says Rebecca. Pappa says I should answer, "Peasant!"

My mouth is full like my mother's. "Where did our mouths come from, Mamma?" She's putting on her lipstick. The color, carnation, is printed in a circle on the bottom.

My mother regards me in the mirror. "The Bermans," she says, her words slurred, her lips stretched across her teeth.

"Can I try some?"

Mamma raises her eyebrows, her brown eyes moving to me again. She relaxes her mouth and closes the tube. "A nine year old doesn't wear lipstick," she answers.

"I'm almost ten," I say quietly.

Mamma blots her lips on a tissue. I can smell the lipstick's perfume. She powders her cheeks. Then she glances at me and smiles. "Grandma Anna says you look like her mother, Yetta—your great grandmother."

Sometimes I look at the black and white pictures of my parents, kept in a big Macy's box on a shelf in the hall closet. Mamma is beautiful with her black curls. Some of the pictures of my mother have half of them cut away. "Whose hand is that at your waist, Mamma?"

"I don't remember," answers my mother.

"Why did you cut the picture?" I ask.

"I didn't," she answers. "Your father did."

In the living room at my grandparents' house on Carroll Street, on a cloth that drapes Aunt Rose's ebony concert piano, there are also pictures. Mamma wearing a dark dress, Pappa a suit, Mamma's head resting on his shoulder. Above them is a print of a painting—a Renoir—a young girl in button-up boots. My parents' eyes shine in the photo lamp, bright against pink photo paper. It was taken when they were young. Now the Renoir hangs in the living room of our house on Crown Street. The girl's hair is red. Her dress is blue.

There are also pictures taken in Vilna, when my grandparents were young. These pictures are sepia-colored and cracked. My grandfather carried them to America in the lining of his coat.

The floor lamp glints off my grandfather's gold wire

glasses, lighting his white, bushy eyebrows, thick as his hair. It lights his suit jacket and his newspaper and casts a shadow on his shoes and the blue carpet. "Anna," he says. "Let me read to you..."

"Sam," my grandmother interrupts softly. "Kinde."

I know this word means 'child.' My grandfather looks at me then turns away. He takes off his glasses and lowers his head. He rubs the red indentations on the bridge of his nose.

My eyes take pictures.

My grandmother's flowered house dress, her face turned toward him. My pale skin and brown eyes reflected in the mirror over the sideboard. At first I don't recognize myself. Snap! The quiet in the room. Snap! The knot in my stomach.

"Come, Mamela," says my grandmother, taking hold of my shoulder. "We'll spiel the cards." She means we'll play them. Her voice is scratchy, her English shaped by the tenements, the Lower East Side of Manhattan. She says "ain't it?" And "yeh!" Words my mother forbids my brothers and sister and me to use.

We pass through the living room to the porch room and settle onto the daybed. "Now we can talk!" says my grandmother quietly, smiling over at me. "Come, we'll spiel Casina."

"Casino, Grandma," I tell her.

"Yeh!" she answers. She takes the deck of cards from a drawer in the table next to the daybed. She sets it on the printed bedspread between us.

"Shuffle them, Mamela," she tells me.

I take the cards from their box. "Low card deals," I say.

"Yeh!" she answers again. She picks the three of spades. I pick the jack of hearts. "Good, Mamela," says my grandmother, taking the deck. "I deal—you'll get the last cards on the table, maybe some points. Good, ain't it?" She looks up and chuckles.

When my grandmother plays Pinochle with my grandfather she wins. She beats Pappa at Casino, sitting forward, glaring at him under her eyebrows. But when she plays with me her face is soft. If she wins she apologizes.

My grandparents' apartment on Carroll Street is two blocks from our house. Aunt Rose, Mamma's sister, lives with my grandparents. Aunt Dorothy, Mamma's other sister lives on Montgomery Street, around the corner from Crown. The rest of Mamma's family lives in The Bronx.

Pappa's family lives in another part of Brooklyn. When they visit they watch the ball game. Then Pappa is quiet. But with Mamma's family, especially my grandmother, he has a lot to say. And he tells jokes, sometimes in English, sometimes in Yiddish. Then Pappa and my grandmother laugh until they cry.

"Sam, a glass of tea?" asks my grandmother. Silence. "He's reading his column, Darling," says my grandmother. My grandfather writes about the labor unions.

My grandmother picks up the cards. "Sam!" she calls again. "It's a beautiful day! The sun is shining, read on the porch!"

My grandfather doesn't answer. Grandma Anna chuckles again. I know she wants to talk about their life before they came here.

The Ruby Ring

Grandma Anna deals us each four cards, and four on the bedspread. Sunlight falls across the piano in the living room next door. It lights a picture of my grandmother, before she came to America, my grandmother's light, braided hair wrapped around her head and pinned at the top. In that picture she's wearing a ring on her third finger. The stone is dark, a ruby. This ring was not given by my grandfather, but by Josef. It was a betrothal, a promise, a match made in Vilna.

"Darling," my grandmother tells me when we play cards. "You'll learn adding and taking away!" And it's then she tells me the stories from Russia.

"I kept the ruby ring hidden," she says. I look at her until she meets my gaze. "We're lucky to be here," says my grandmother. "Spiel, Mamela, play the cards, Sweetheart!" She looks over at the picture of herself. "I wore it—when it seemed safe." She shrugs. "The Cossacks would have taken it if they'd seen it."

A feeling starts in my legs and goes up my back. Snap!

"Got a tvey? A two? Take my two—the good two, a point for you, my darling."

I win the first round. My grandmother deals again. Twenty-one points makes a winner. Eleven points to a game. Sometimes it takes two games, sometimes three, for one of us to win.

"Josef kept the Sabbath. But not your grandfather. You got a tsen, Ruthie?"

"Ten, Grandma," I tell her. "Yeh, tsen," she answers. Then she tells me that one night my grandfather came to her home in Vilna. "People from everywhere came to see my father," she tells me. "He was a scholar. My mother opened the door. 'Sam Bailenson' he said, introducing himself. It was as if I'd been waiting to hear that name all my life."

"My father was in his study. I heard the words—'the murder of the Jews!'" and her eyes are so far away that she can't see me. "'We have to take things into our own hands!' said your grandfather. 'The Messiah won't come by revolution' my father answered."

"Ruthie—Mamela—I'm sorry—." She touches my cheek. The sun seems too bright through the windows. She looks down at her cards. She picks one out and puts it on the table. It's the good ten, worth two points, the most valuable card in the game. "You got a tsen, take it." she says.

"Ten, Grandma," I tell her softly.

"Yeh!" she answers. "Ten," she says carefully.

I take the good ten with the ten of clubs and the game is mine.

"Lucky in cards, lucky in love!" says my grandmother, reaching, cradling my face in her hands.

"Like you," I say.

She looks surprised. Then she smiles. "I went to hear him speak and waited for him. He walked me home. I stopped to look up at the stars. Suddenly he lifted me off the ground. 'Get a better look!' he said." She looks at me and shakes her head. "What could I do? I gave back the ruby ring and told my mother. She gave me her wedding veil..." she stops. I see that the wrinkles under her eyes are wet. "Your great grandfather, my father, said the kaddish, the prayer for the dead."

I reach for my grandmother's hand. She lifts my hand to her cheek. Then we both look up. My grandfather is standing at the door. He bends to kiss me.

"Lucky in love?" says my grandmother. "You're here, Ruthie!"

For Ruthie

"Is that why you left? Is that why you came here?" I ask.

My grandfather has sat down with his newspaper

again.

"I wanted to go to Palestine," says my grandmother. "But your grandfather had a friend here." My grandmother's blue eyes look far away. Again they fill with tears. She sniffs. "There's a tree there with your name on it, Mamela." Maybe you'll get there someday. Maybe you'll go and see it." My grandmother packs up the cards and puts them back in the drawer. She sighs.

"Come, Sam," she says. "We'll have a glass of tea and tell Ruthie how we came to America, it's her history." She starts toward the kitchen and I follow.

My grandfather frowns and answers in Yiddish. I hear the word 'kinde.'

My grandmother's answer is a mix of languages. She's shaking her head, arguing with my grandfather. "So who will tell her?" she finishes in English. "Ruthie's growing up," she says looking at me. She waits for me to catch up and puts her arm around my shoulder.

In the kitchen she puts the kettle on to boil.

"It began with two soldiers—and a printing press. Your grandfather's. They came to the house in Vilna, looking for it."

My grandfather sits down with us. "Somebody told them," he says quietly.

"Your grandfather wrote articles. He wanted people to organize, to fight back. He printed the names of people the Czar had murdered." She's looking out the window where the big leaves of the elephant ear tree grow close to the glass.

My grandfather and I look at each other. He opens his mouth as if he wants to say something but he doesn't. Grandma Anna gets up. She crosses the room and opens the dish cabinet. She takes out three plates and brings them to the table. At the sink she rinses spoons. From the silverware drawer she takes forks and a knife. She picks

24

up the metal napkin holder then changes her mind and puts it down.

Instead she opens the lid on the polished wood box where folded linen napkins are kept, to use for occasions.

"One soldier stayed outside with the horses. The other came in." She sits down. "Snow was falling. The horses were stamping." My grandparents look at each other. My grandmother sighs and looks away.

"The boy stood between us," says my grandfather. My grandmother nods. "He looked around the room—"

Grandma Anna laughs. "What did we have? A stove, a table, our bed, books, a picture on the wall of—a man—and the rug under my feet, covering the hatch in the floor."

"He turned back to the picture. I held my breath."

"Who is that?" he asked your grandfather. I answered fast. 'My uncle,'" I said. The soldier crossed the room and knocked the picture to the floor. The glass shattered. A drop of blood appeared on his knuckle. He had cut himself!"

"Now he was angry. He turned to me. He came this near," says my grandmother. "I could feel his breath. I didn't move. I didn't want the floor to creak!"

"The colors in that rug shone up at me, laying over the trap door, over the printing press!"

My grandfather looks at me. His eyes are like mine, brown and dark and open, filling the room. My grandmother glances at him, then she looks at me.

"That's when I smiled, Ruthie!" she says.

I let out my breath. "You—smiled?" I repeat.

"Yes," she answers and laughs.

"The other soldier came to the door, three faces looked inside, his and the two horses!"

"They were cold," says my grandfather. His eyes are

25

lidded, angry.

"I offered them a glass of tea, and some honey cake," says my grandmother.

"My heart was beating. I turned and walked to the stove where the honey cake sat, still warm. I picked it up and was about to set it on the table. Then, you know what? The first one grabbed it, pan and all!"

"One minute they were there, the next they were gone! It was my mother's recipe."

"They were starving!" says my grandfather.

"We stood there in the silence. Then we packed our clothes. We left that night and never went back. The printing press stayed where it was, in the floor!"

"But who would have told them?" I ask.

"Who? Who knows? Maybe someone—"

"—Josef." My grandfather says quietly.

Inside me are pictures: The wrinkles in my grandmother's cheeks, running with tears; her embroidered handkerchief, wiping her eyes. My grandfather turning toward the window, looking far away, then turning toward me. My shoulder feeling warm, pressed against him.

My grandmother gets up and takes my face in her hands. "Mamela," she says. Then she bends and kisses me, her cheek cool and damp. "Let me get the cake." She crosses the kitchen to the counter.

"What uncle was it, Grandma?" I ask.

"Uncle?" she repeats, pouring out the tea. "What uncle?"

"In the picture—on the wall."

"Oh! That uncle!"

"It was Uncle Karl," answers my grandfather. "Uncle

Karl Marx."

The kitchen is silent. Then my grandparents begin to laugh.

"Karl Marx?" I'm asking. "Of Marxism?"

"Yes, that Karl Marx," answers my grandmother.

My grandfather could be the Czar's brother. "A dead ringer," says my brother Leon. "But look at the eyes."

I once saw a picture. The Czar's eyes were pale, small, looking at nothing. My grandfather's seem to look right through you.

Grandma Anna serves the tea. She takes a honey cake out of the breadbox and brings it to the table. "This one is for us," she tells my grandfather, cutting three pieces. "And for Ruthie."

"Na, Ruthie, here. Your Great Grandma Yetta's recipe."

I look at her, wide-eyed.

"Yeh!" she says. "I'll teach it to you, Ruthela. That would make her so happy!"

"Eat, Sam, Ruthie. Es! Azai goot! I baked it this morning. Taste it. It tastes so sweet!"

We eat in silence, the cake still warm.

My grandfather sits, handsome, proud, a prince grown old.

The Czar and his family were murdered after my grandparents fled to America. But others, like my great grandparents, stayed. I see them in dreams, people I never knew. Those dreams wake me, and Pappa stays until I can sleep again.

My grandparents came to America with thousands of other Jews fleeing persecution—the massacres—the Czar's pogroms. They left that night for Minsk. My grandmother sailed for America, my grandfather came a

year later.
    And if they hadn't I wouldn't be here.

BOOK TWO

Benny Pitt

"Ruthie!" shouts Mamma from the living room. "Don't lock yourself in your room. Answer the telephone, I've got an apron full of glass!"

"Okay, Mamma!" I answer.

I hurry past my collections shelf, the place where rows of boxes and cans sit, filled with rocks, things I've found in the street, my horse rein, my charm collection, and the cookie tin where I keep my fat collection, when I can manage to get some fat, and then to carry it past my mother and Rebecca, my sister, without them noticing. Fat from the butcher—Benny Pitt's—though I can only keep that fat there on my collection shelf to enjoy for an afternoon, opening and closing the cookie tin to turn it over in my hands and sniff it, before putting it outside. By then it isn't white as cut marble the way it was when Benny Pitt trimmed it from its meat. And generally it's begun to smell.

I open the door. "I'll be right back," I whisper to my doll, Hannah, then hurry to get the telephone.

"It's Mrs. Lamont, Ruthie, is your sister, Rebecca, there?" But Rebecca is out with Sam. "Will you tell her I need her to baby sit Saturday night? Thanks, Ruthie."

In the living room I tell my mother about Mrs. Lamont. My mother is sitting on the floor. Cradled in her lap is a crystal lampshade that belongs to the dining room chandelier. She's rubbing it clean with a soft cotton rag—Georgie's old diaper. Tarnished brass, a jar of polish,

29

vinegar, more old diapers sit on big open sheets of The New York Times. "Rebecca is babysitting for your brother Saturday night," answers my mother.

"I can baby sit for Georgie, Mamma."

"When you're ten you can baby sit for Georgie," she says without looking up.

"Evy Mailman baby sits for her sister," I say.

Now Mamma's brown eyes catch mine. "Evy's sister isn't your brother," she answers. "And Evy's aunt lives upstairs."

"Aunt Dorothy is around the corner," I answer. My mother scowls. "Here," she says, handing me shreds of Georgie's diaper. "I need your help."

"But Mamma—Hannah's waiting for me." I say it softly. My cheeks get hot.

My mother inspects me over her glasses. Her frown softens. "A doll can wait, the housework can't," she says without lowering her voice.

"Mamma—please!" I look toward the door of Rebecca's room, as if the words will hang in the air until she and Sam get back from the skating rink. Then she'd call me an infant. I sit down on the rug beside my mother. "I need a job too."

Now my mother is looking at me. Her eyes seem so dark and brown I can't turn away. "A nine year old doesn't work," she says.

"Mamma, I'm nine and three quarters," I say, pulling my eyes from her gaze. I moisten the rag with polish and rub the brass until it flashes in the reading lamp. But her eyes are on me, I can feel them. "Don't leave streaks," says my mother. She turns away but I catch her smile. "You're a great help, Ruthela," she says quietly. "Come, we'll finish quickly. I have to go to the butcher's for fricassee."

"Mamma—if I had a job I could save money."

"And why should you need money?" exclaims my mother, laying Georgie's diaper in her lap. Now she's taken her glasses off to look at me.

"Hannah—needs something—uh—new," I answer. "There's a doll carriage set in Bender's window—." I'm biting my lip.

In the toy window of Bender's Department Store, on Schenectady Avenue, is a yellow knitted carriage set. It has a blanket, a pillow cover and a matching sweater, with ribbon ties. And two tortoise shell plastic clips.

"It's so perfect, Mamma! It's like the one Joannie Nevins's sister has in green!"

My mother sighs. She picks up the glass shade, holds it with Georgie's diaper, turns it in front of the reading lamp. She scowls and rubs out a tiny blemish.

"Mamma, it's three dollars and fifty cents—I could ask Mrs. Greene if she could hire me to watch the twins—or clean her house—"

"Clean her house—!" Mamma's face flushes as she turns to me. First she's silent. Then she says, "My children don't clean houses—they go to school!" She's speaking quietly, but the sorrow in her eyes stops my breath. It presses down on my chest. Then I am caught by surprise, because my mother puts the glass she's polishing in her lap and reaches for me. She pulls me to her and kisses my head. "Here there are laws," she says. "And labor unions. Thank God—and people like your grandfather who organize them!"

"Ruthela," she says, then she's silent. And for a terrible minute I think my mother is going to cry. But she lets me go, sighs and picks up the glass shade. She seems frail, tired. A silence falls between us. I finish one brass fitting then a second. Mamma rubs the glass. There's a

31

tight feeling in my throat.

When the work is done I stand on a kitchen chair and we put the chandelier back together. My mother sighs again then looks at me. "There's plenty of work here," says my mother. "Thank you, Sweetheart—I'm grateful for your help."

In my room I take Hannah from the high chair that used to be Rebecca's, then Leon's, then mine, then Georgie's. I take off Hannah's jumper, dress her in Georgie's old pajamas and lay her in her box for a nap. I cover her with the blanket that my grandmother crocheted for Rebecca. When Georgie was born, Mamma sewed new gray satin ribbons on the edges to match the color, but Leon told me it was green when it was his. "I'll bring you something back," I whisper to Hannah, taking a nickel from Pappa's red Revelation pipe tobacco tin, where I keep my allowance.

Mamma knocks softly at my door. She's changed to a skirt and blouse, her nylon seamed stockings and suede street shoes. "Come, Ruthie, we'll go to Benny Pitt's, quickly before Georgie wakes up." She taps Leon's door as she passes. Leon's head pokes around the door frame. "Help Georgie if he needs anything," Mamma whispers. "Your father is writing!" "Mamma, I've got a final exam!" says my brother. "Shh!" says my mother. "You'll wake your brother. We won't be long." I glance back at Leon. His face is turned to the door. His eyes are shut.

We start down Crown Street. "What a help you are to me, Ruthie," Mamma says and, at last, smiles brightly. We round the corner to Troy Avenue and pass Kogen's Drug Store. Inside I can see the Kogen brothers. One is behind the counter, the other is sweeping the floor. The Kogen brothers are twins.

They have the same gray hair and the same kind of silver wire glasses. But one of them is bigger than the other. "Which one is Simon and which one is Abe, Mamma?"

"Shh!" she says, giving me a fierce look. "Who gave you permission to call adults by their first names?" She glances through the big store window. "That one is Abe," she whispers when we clear the door. She holds her hand in front of her stomach and makes a curve.

Benny Pitt owns the butcher shop on Troy Avenue. His floor is covered with fresh sawdust. His glass cases are filled with ice and neat rows of sliced steaks and chops. When Mamma sends Rebecca to pick up meat for supper, Rebecca begs my mother to send me or Leon. Rebecca doesn't eat meat. "The smell makes me sick, Mamma!" she says. But I like the smell of Benny Pitt's butcher shop—the woody, sappy sawdust, the chicken fat, the greasy, garlicky salami and the full, good smell of raw meat. I like watching Benny Pitt chop a chicken into eighths for soup and trim fat off lamb and beef, smartly, with his sharp knife—pieces that are white and tidy as soap. "Suet," says Benny Pitt. "The birds l-o-o-ve it, Dahling, and who can blame them?" In first grade Mrs. Wolfsen asked us what we wanted to be when we grew up. I said I wanted to be a butcher like Benny Pitt. Steven Berman told Aylene Muntzer who told everyone on Crown Street. Pappa told me to call them all peasants. "A butcher makes a nice living," said my father.

The bells on Benny Pitt's door jingle as it opens. "Hello, Mrs. Pincus, hello, Ruthie!" Benny Pitt smiles from behind his wooden block. His red cheeks look like ripe apples. Winter and summer he wears a woolen cap to cover his shiny head and fringe of hair in the cold of the meat refrigerator. "I have some nice fat for you, Ruthie!" he declares now. "For your collection!"

Benny Pitt knows I like to collect fat. He knows that last winter I kept it in a cookie tin in the back yard by the Rose of Sharon bush. He knows because he asked me if I'd like to have some when I couldn't take my eyes off it as he trimmed it from Mamma's beef stew the first time Mamma sent me to the butcher by myself. Sometimes he gives me a waxed paper bagful and I keep it in the tin until it starts to smell. Then I put it out in the alley for the stray cats. But when it's fresh and sitting in the cookie tin it looks like something sweet for dessert.

"You can put it out for the birds!" says Benny Pitt now. "Nice, sweet fat!" My walking slows and I look down at the sawdust. "Uh—I'm not—uh—collecting today." Then I look at my mother. Mamma is looking at Benny Pitt, shaking her head.

"No?" Benny Pitt asks softly. "What's the matter?"

My thoughts start racing: Benny-Pitt-I-wish-I-could-take-that-fat-wrapped-in-a-bundle-like-white-chocolate-I-don't-care-that-Rebecca-got-upset-when-she-found-out-about-my-fat-collection-and-told-Mamma-I-have-a-problem. "Uh—thank you—I mean—um—no thank you!" I tell him instead. My cheeks are stinging hot.

"—Have you got a nice soup chicken?" Mamma interrupts. "Not too big!" she says. "And fresh!"

Benny Pitt hurries to the back of the store where the silver refrigerator lines the wall. He opens the door. "Only fresh!" he declares in puffs of steam. "Dah-ling!" tilting his head from one side to the other. "A good soup this will make!" His voice gets muffled as he disappears inside the refrigerator. Then he reappears holding the chicken by its feet. Starting back toward us he slams the door closed behind him with his foot.

I flash to the chickens at the farm down the road from Miller's Bungalow Colony, where we stayed one summer. Rebecca and I fed them corn. I remember how one of them looked up at me with its black bird eyes, tilting its little head, as if to say thank you. This one's eyes are closed. It has no feathers. My stomach knots up. My sister won't eat chicken, not even Mamma's chicken soup. But I can't imagine going without Mamma's chicken soup, loaded with feet, searching for the hen's eggs that haven't grown shells yet. I try to banish the picture of the black and white feathers on the chickens at Miller's from my mind. And the tiny yellow downy chicks that hatch from their eggs. This chicken's floppy and looks like it's rubber, but it isn't.

"Not too big!" Benny Pitt is saying, repeating Mamma's command, "And swe–eeet, Dahling, like sugar! I'll give you extra feet." "How disgusting!" my sister will scream. "I can't look at them, Mamma!" Georgie thinks they're funny. My mother saves them for me. I prefer them to ice cream or malomars or sugar daddies, though I can't eat them in school or on the way home or sitting on the stoop. Aylene and Joannie Nevins wouldn't understand. Benny Pitt snaps a sheet of paper from its roll, wraps the chicken and puts it into a bag. "And what else?" he asks, his cheeks red and smiling.

"Two pounds chop meat—no fat!" says my mother.

"No!" he agrees. His knife flies while my mother watches over her glasses. "Fresh, lean, lean, fresh," he's murmuring, trimming fat. "Sweet, sweet, sweet!" he declares. He presses the meat into the grinder. Strings of hamburger fall onto the paper in his hand.

From the ceiling of the butcher shop hangs a row of kosher salamis. As the meat grinder whines I count nine.

"Can we get a salami, Mamma?" I ask. My mother leans closer and frowns. I point, "can we get a salami?" But she's distracted, turning to see the chop meat piling higher in Benny Pitt's white paper. "Mamma, a salami? Can we GET ONE?" The butcher has switched off the meat grinder and the last words fill the butcher shop. Mamma looks furious. Her mouth is pinched.

When my mother buys a salami it doesn't last long. She used to hide it at the back of the refrigerator, behind my father's ptcha—jellied cows feet, or his borscht, things that confuse Georgie and make him wretch and even I won't eat. But my brothers found the salami anyway. "Salami isn't dessert! It's lunch for a week!" said my mother. But it may as well be dessert. Mamma hid the next salami in a cooking pot on the porch. It was winter. Sandra Bender's dog, Mitzi, found it. Once she put one in the kitchen drawer so that Georgie wouldn't see it until she could hide it. But Mamma forgot and it spoiled. The smell of rotten meat and garlic made Rebecca sick and she stayed at Aunt Dorothy's until the house aired out. "We have enough to eat!" she says under her breath now.

"And next time," says Benny Pitt, "a salami, yes, Dahling?" he winks at me as my mother pays him. "Enjoy, Dahling," he says, handing the bag to me. As we leave, Moshe comes in and tips his hat to Mamma and me. Moshe delivers meat for Benny Pitt.

We stop at Finder's Grocery and Mamma shops for fruit and vegetables. "You're a big help, Ruthie," she tells me again as we leave Finder's. She sighs. We walk down Montgomery Street and up Schenectady Avenue to Young's Laundry for my father's shirts. "I wonder how Georgie is..." Mamma is saying as we pass Bender's.

"Wait, Mamma..." I look into Bender's window. The knitted

carriage set isn't there. My feet seem stuck to the sidewalk in front of Bender's window. Then a terrifying thought shoots through me. It's been sold! I'm searching the window with my eyes. The only thing yellow is a pair of pedal pushers!

Now my mother turns to me. I turn to her. Her face looks blurred and I turn back toward the window. Mamma pulls a handkerchief from her purse and stuffs it into my hand. I hold it to my eyes. She looks into Bender's window too. She doesn't say "come we have to hurry because your brother is a lunatic when he first wakes up and if he doesn't see me he'll make Leon a lunatic and your father won't be able to work!" Instead she moves toward Bender's door. "Well it won't hurt to ask," she says, and pushes the door open.

Mrs. Bender is folding sweaters, kneeling in the aisle between two display racks of shirts and blouses. She nods to us. Mr. Bender smiles to my mother from behind a counter. "How are you, Mrs. Pincus, can I help you?" His eyes shift to me and he nods without saying anything.

"We were wondering about the doll carriage set," says Mamma. Her eyebrows are arched, her lids are half closed.

"The doll carriage set?" repeats Mr. Bender.

"It was in your window," says my mother.

"The window?" says Mr. Bender.

"It—it's yellow," I say.

"Yellow?" he echoes.

"It's in the middle drawer!" calls Mrs. Bender.

Mr. Bender opens a drawer behind the counter. When his hand comes up it's holding the yellow carriage set. I rest Pappa's shirts on the counter and touch the wool.

"It's reduced!" Mrs. Bender calls. "It's dusty." The she turns to us. "Just a little—from being in the window," she explains to my mother. "It's half price."

37

My heart starts pounding.

"Half price?" Mr. Bender repeats to his wife. Then he turns back to my mother. "That makes it—"

"—a dollar seventy five." says my mother.

"A dollar seventy five," says Mr. Bender.

I look over at my mother. Her eyes are on Mr. Bender as she snaps open her purse. Then she looks down and takes out fifty cents. "We'd like to hold it," she says.

"Hold it?" says Mr. Bender. "It's a sale item—"

"We'll hold it for a week!" calls Mrs. Bender.

"That will be fine," says my mother.

I bite my lip while Mr. Bender writes "Hold For Pincus" on a slip of paper and pins it to the tag.

"But Mamma, how—?" I begin as we hurry up Schenectady Avenue.

"Georgie must be a wreck!" my mother is saying. "He'll drive your brother crazy. Your father has a deadline, come, Ruthie!"

"Mamma, my birthday isn't for three months!"

"You think I don't know? Your father needs to eat, come!"

"Mamma, if—if I could earn money...!" I call, walking quickly to keep up with her.

"Children don't work in America!" calls my mother her heels beating staccato on the concrete. "Anything can happen in a week. We'll see!"

A week, a week, a week! I'm thinking. Seven days! We reach the corner of Crown Street, Nat's Candy Store and the row of glass machines with the one that has toys. I feel for the nickel in my pocket. I promised Hannah. But that was before Bender's, before my mother put a down payment on the carriage set. My mother is walking fast, turning into Crown Street.

"Georgie gets crazy!" my mother is shouting to the sky.

I put the nickel back in my pocket.

Collector

I'm feeding Hannah lunch. What can I do for the Science Fair project, I'm asking myself. What can I do what can I do what can I do and be finished in two weeks? It isn't long enough to think of something and then do it, I'm saying inside. Why doesn't Mrs. Roth ever give us enough time?

"Ruthie!" calls my mother. "Enough hiding in your room when the sun is shining! Come with me to the butcher, you'll help me carry the bags."

Just when Hannah is settled into her high chair and I've mixed up talcum powder and toothpaste to look like rice cereal for her lunch, my mother is calling me.

"What are you doing, wasting food?" She says when I hope she won't notice the leftovers I'd rather use for Hannah's lunch, wrapped in my napkin from the table, sitting in the fold of my sweater in my lap. I can't eat anymore, I tell her then. "Yes you can," she answers, "some children have nothing to eat. The gentiles," she tells my father, "the gentiles." Tells it to him using the Yiddish. "If it isn't finished for supper their children eat it for breakfast. The goyum don't waste food!"

The image of people called gentiles sits in the air. What do they look like? I think of them eating cold spaghetti for breakfast. I feel sorry about this, and my stomach knots, and I consider letting my food get cold before I eat it, in solidarity with the gentiles—in solidarity with the goyum. Then the air in the kitchen feels heavy

39

and Pappa looks uncomfortable. "Eat Ruthela," he says then. "Sit, Miriam. Sit down and eat too."

I remember the first time I knowingly laid eyes on someone who wasn't Jewish. She came to the door, a neighbor. She had a nose, a mouth, soft eyes. She smiled at Mamma. Then she looked at me and smiled again, and I loved her. How could she not be Jewish? I thought. But Mamma had whispered it to my father. How? How? How? Buzzed like an electric saw, like a mosquito in my mind, until my head felt blank and empty and began to hurt and I had to stop thinking about it.

"Now, Ruthie!" Mamma calls, knocking at the door of my room.

At Benny Pitt's I watch as he trims the fat from the beef my mother is buying for stew. A small, white pile grows on his wooden block, a pile so tasty looking, it could be a mound of candy, or halvah, or something exotic from some other country, say Mongolia or French Canada, or bits of soap from Paris.

Benny Pitt sweeps the pile of fat up with his knife. He drops it into the garbage pail. He trims some more, and drops the pieces into his pail. Cut, cut, scoop, plunk, into the pail. Cut, cut—his knife stops, while I'm thinking, All that good fat, what a waste!

Benny Pitt looks at me. His eyes are asking: Are you collecting again? I shake my head.

Recently I've stopped collecting fat, after having left it out in the milk box so that it wouldn't smell. The milkman objected to its being there. He told Mamma that the Health Department frowned on anything sharing a milk box, particularly fat.

Cut, cut, plunk! goes Benny Pitt's knife. Now he really looks at me. "Would you like some for the birds, Ruthie?" he asks. I realize I'm frowning. In my peripheral vision I'm suddenly aware of my mother. I shift my eyes as far as they'll go without turning my head. Even without looking directly at her I can see her pink cheeks. I feel myself flush too.

"It's suet, Mrs. Pincus. The birds love it! Oh how they l-o-v-e it, Dahling!" Benny Pitt is looking at my mother, waiting for her to agree, but she's stiff, her elbow is pushing against my arm. Benny Pitt's forehead is shining. He lowers his glance, takes another piece of meat and trims the fat. His knife cuts like a razor, making surfaces that glisten like the quartz crystal in my rock collection. I try to keep my eyes from looking at the small white hill of fat cubes but I can't. Benny Pitt eases his knife under it, turns toward the garbage pail and leans. He looks up. Our eyes meet. He looks back down at the fat. He's still turned, forming a diagonal between his wooden block and the brown paper lined silver pail. Again he looks at me, then at the fat. Then fast at me, then the pail, almost at the same time. Then his eyes seem focused on both of us at once. Me. The pail. Me. Then he leans on the counter. "Ruthie, Dahling—would you like to have it? You'll put it outside in your back yard for the sparrows!"

In my peripheral vision my mother is shaking her head. Then we talk at the same time. "Yes!" I say. "No!" says my mother. Now Benny Pitt looks from Mamma to me, me to Mamma. I'm nodding, she's shaking her head. Benny Pitt's head is moving too, up and down, nodding, then side to side, making a kind of circle until he shakes himself as if he's waking up from a dream. Then he slips the fat quickly into a waxed paper bag. "The birds will

41

enjoy it!" he apologizes to my mother. "Suet," he's murmuring, now to himself. "How the birds love it!" he says, his apple cheeks shining.

Mamma's face is angry behind the brown paper bag she's carrying as we hurry home. She looks straight ahead. Her heels click sharply against the pavement.

"Mamma you said—you said—it isn't right to waste food..."

My mother stops walking. She glares at me. "It isn't right when people are starving!" she answers. "Birds can find their own food!"

"Mamma, it's cold. Where can you find bugs in winter? Besides, it looks too—interesting to—to just throw away!"

My mother opens her mouth then closes it. "What does?" she says next. I'm silent. "The fat?" she asks. "The fat looks interesting?" I look at her. People pass us on the street. "Mamma—it looks—a certain way. A way that makes you not want to throw it away." My cheeks are hot.

"Come, Ruthela," my mother says quietly. "Your father will be hungry." She walks slower. Her heels are soft on the concrete. I hear her sigh.

I take everything off my collection shelf, which stands in the corner between Hannah's cardboard crib and my dresser. I stack the two boxes that once were filled with my Uncle Harold's cigars but are now filled with trading cards, twice as many as last year, when my sister, Rebecca, gave me hers. "How can you just give them to me?" I asked in disbelief. Rebecca just shrugged. After struggling with her for three years to get her to trade the poodles she just gives me her whole collection. It's Sam. Since Sam and Rebecca talked about getting engaged my sister is different. "Who will I trade with?" I asked her. "Your friends," she answered. I just

42

stared at her.

Even having a full set of poodles, green, pink and blue, nearly impossible to find anywhere, there's a queasy feeling in my stomach when I look at them. "How can you play with these? They have no numbers." my brother, Georgie, asked. "You don't play with them, you collect them," I told him. "What for?" asked Georgie next. "They're trading cards, Georgie. You trade them," I said. "But they're empty—who would want them?" said Georgie. "Donna would," I told Georgie, trying to be patient, trying not to sound annoyed, trying not to make him cry. Then I ignored him.

But ignoring Georgie is never productive. Next he complained that trading cards are stupid, that they are not like pictures of baseball players. "What are these?" asked Georgie next, nudging the ballet dancers set I'd lined up to look at, "What ar-rrr-rre theyyy?"

"Georgie!" I said.

"I don't underrr-st-aaannnd!" said Georgie. Then he started to cry. Georgie is sensitive. "Look, Georgie," I said, really trying, showing him the turtles and the swordfish. "These are interesting, aren't they?" And this worked for a few minutes. He sniffed and wiped his cheeks with his hands. I offered him a tissue. He accepted it.

"Can I have them?" he asked next.

"No, Georgie, I need them!" I answered.

Georgie's eyes filled up again. "But why?" he asked, his chin quivering.

"To trade," I answered as gently as I could.

"But they don't have any num—bbers!" Georgie's face screwed up and I knew what was coming.

"It's a set, Georgie," I told him. "It's valuable—" But it was too late.

"Maa-mma! MAA-MAA!" my brother Georgie was

screaming, running down the hallway. "MAA-MAAA IT'S NOT LIKE THEY HAVE NUM—BERS ON THEM!"

"Georgie, you need a nap!" said my mother.

"But you can't play with them, they're emm—pty!" Georgie tried to explain to her.

"Come Sweetheart," said Mamma. "Help me with the stew." But Georgie was crying at the top of his lungs. "Here, Georgie, wash the turnips for me."

"But MAMM—MMA!"

"GEORGIE!" my mother shouted suddenly. Then the house was quiet. When I heard my mother singing I knew my brother was either washing turnips or he'd fallen asleep on the kitchen linoleum.

Next I dust the cover of my dog picture album, which I've kept since first grade.

Every breed is labeled with names I've typed on Pappa's old typewriter. It doesn't type n's so I use the m's instead. "Dobermam Pimscher?" asked Leon. I just looked at him.

"Pappa's typewriter," said my brother. Leon used to type his papers on it until he bought another one, second hand, with the money he earned working after school at Finder's Grocery. I turn the album's pages, remembering the afternoons spent with Maxie Fuller and Rona Buxbaum, hunting for pictures of Lhasa Apsos and Basenjis. Until Maxie found hers in a library book and cut them out. I told Mamma and that was the end of our dog picture meetings. My parents talked about it in Yiddish. The words I recognized were "Maxie" and "Rona." Leon, who understands Yiddish, said he couldn't believe a nine-year-old would do that. He called it desecration. "A book is sacred," said my father when he tucked me in that night. Aunt Rose believed Maxie would do it. She said she didn't think I should be friends with her. She called it stealing. My Aunt Rose is a straight talker. She's the one who speaks English when the other grownups are speaking Yiddish. "Rose, shah!" says my Aunt Dorothy, or my grandmother, or Mamma, then. "Shah! Kinder! Children!" Then Aunt Rose looks around at us and winks.

In two coffee cans at the bottom of my collection shelf are things I've found in the street. Flattened jar tops, pieces of rusty machinery, sardine cans. Some are things I can't identify that look interesting corroded and flattened. Things I've picked up on my way to school, or shopping for my mother, things run over by car wheels, looking like sunsets, or beach scenes or faces. Like the goldfish face that used to be part of a can opener.

"My God! What is this?" asked my mother when she found the sardines can in my jacket pocket.

"It's for my collection," I said.

"What collection?" Mamma asked.

"My Things-found-in-the-street-that-uh-look-interesting collection," I answered.

My mother looked at me. I looked at her. First she frowned. Then her lips moved, as if she were about to say something. Then her shoulders sagged. Suddenly she touched my face, softly. "Wash it, Ruthie," she said. "Use soap, Darling, and the nailbrush." Later my parents spoke in Yiddish. "Germs," my mother said in English. But I could tell from my father's tone that he was defending me. He said the word "artistic." In English. My mother said something about Aunt Rose.

"How would you like to trip and fall?" my mother asks

45

when we walk together in the street and I'm looking down at the sidewalk to see what's there—shells in the concrete. Or names. Or words, like "Spitz was here," in the pavement in front of Aylene Muntzer's. And sometimes there are rusted objects, an old key, a nail, a bolt, pieces that have fallen off someone's bike or a baby's carriage, things that are still perfectly good that I need for my collection. Then I wait until Mamma walks ahead and pick them up.

Aunt Dorothy tells Mamma I'm a collector. She said it in the kitchen the day I brought home the insides of someone's watch which I found half buried in the dirt around the hedge in front of Mr. Solloway's house. I heard them talking from the bathroom where I was washing it off, admiring the way part of it was rusted orange and part of it was gleaming in the bathroom light as I rubbed it dry. "A garbage collector!" I heard my mother say. "Miriam," I heard my aunt answer, "Someday she'll collect antiques and make a nice living." "Do you think so?" I heard my mother ask.

I empty Benny Pitt's waxed bag of fat into the cookie tin on my collection shelf, next to my charm collection. It just fits.

Fat

My parents are talking in the kitchen, looking at the pages of a magazine lying open on the table.

"But what is it, David?" my mother is asking my father. I can hear her through the doorway of my room.

"It's a sculpture," my father answers. "It's in the museum."

"The museum!" exclaims my mother, then she takes

46

off in Yiddish, but finishes in English. "Junk!" she says.

"Right!" agrees my father. "You look at it, I look at it, and that's what we see. Pablo Picasso, he sees something else." Then Pappa reads from the magazine. "Picasso frequents Parisian junkyards seeking things that inspire him. He collects these things to use in his sculptures." Pappa chuckles. "Sound familiar?" he asks my mother.

"He collects junk!" says Mamma. Then, silence.

"Miriam, stop worrying," says my father.

I walk down to the kitchen and stand in the doorway. Mamma is examining the magazine. She holds it up, close to her face. "It looks like a goat—or maybe—a deer," she's saying. "The greatest living artist," she reads. "Three-hundred-thousand dollars a museum pays?! With people in Europe starving?" she asks with disgust.

"Miriam, Ruthie has enough to eat. Assemb-laaage," reads my father.

"Pablo," says my mother.

"Picasso," answers my father. "It's a talent, Miriam. A gift. An artist is a—kind of person! Assem-blaaage," he says again.

"A junk dealer!" says my mother. She sees me and flushes.

"Junk?" I repeat. "Can I see?"

Pappa's chair creaks as he looks around. My mother sits up straight. I slide between the table and Mamma. "Picasso," I read, tracing the letters with my finger. "It's an—antelope!" I look at the rusted handlebars in the picture. "He used them for horns!"

My God! My God! My God! It's gorgeous! I'm thinking.

"An antelope," my mother is repeating. "How do you know?"

"It says so, Mamma! He put two things together from a bicycle someone threw away! The seat and the handlebars made an animal!"

"It's rusty," says my mother.

Inside I've begun dancing. I'm standing still but my feet are flying around the kitchen, my shoes skidding on the yellow linoleum. My insides feel like Mexican jumping beans, like balloons, tugging at their strings, breaking free, making their way to the sky. Two thrown-away things! Things no one wanted just tossed into the garbage!

"The rust is beautiful!" I almost shout. "And no one noticed it but Pablo Picasso! Those things would have just been wasted, Mamma! Mamma, it's just another kind of food!"

Pappa smiles. Mamma sighs. She looks tired. "I hope he gives his money to charity," she says.

Before I go to bed I walk back to the kitchen. Pablo Picasso's black eyes look right at me from the table. A mist of white hair crowns his head. "Pablo," I say out loud.

"Pablo Pablo Pablo Pablo," feeling like I'd like to go outside into the dark night, saying his name, skipping down Crown Street while cars pass whispering over the cobblestones. Pablo Pablo Pablo, music rising, bouncing off the lit windows, off the glowing crescent moon.

"Pablo!" I whisper to the wide black eyes in the picture. The sound hangs in the air over the kitchen table. Floats there as if it's answering, Ruthie! I touch the pages of the article. I can't believe how beautiful the sculptures are. Picasso sculpts with found objects, I read. Found objects! Like my sardines can and watch insides and flattened can opener that sit in the can on my collection shelf! Pablo Picasso would understand.

I start to laugh. It flutters up from my chest, a laugh I don't recognize, as if it's coming from someone I never met before. Then my eyes sting with tears and my throat feels tight, and Pappa comes into the kitchen. He's looking over my shoulder at the magazine. I'm pinching my lips tight, my hands on the photographs of Pablo's sculptures.

My father bends down. He's looking at the photographs too. Then he's looking at me. I'm sniffing. I turn to look at my father. He's smiling. "Ruthie," he says softly. "You're an artist."

An artist. Donna Pukatch says the same thing. And so does Aunt Rose. It's true that when I press my soft, black math pencil into paper I love the way it feels. Mrs. Roth says I press too hard. But I love the way the paper curls from all those black carved numbers. And I love the way my lines curve—lines that are extra, lines that aren't numbers, aren't words, aren't anything but lines I can't help drawing with that black pencil on the pulpy yellow, lined math paper. I love the way those lines curve around the math examples. Then my ears close, and I'm not in school, not anywhere but in those lines. Mrs. Roth draws red Xs next to those lines on my homework, which upsets my parents. But I could draw all day.

I bring the magazine back to my room, put it on my dresser where I can see Pablo's picture, go to my collection shelf and get down the coffee can of things found in the street. I pick out the watch gears. The overhead light catches the scratch marks on the brass. He'd like this too, I'm thinking, and I wish I could talk to him about it. If I hadn't picked it up the street cleaner would have swept it into his trash bin. What a waste! What a waste, I'd tell Pablo. Out the window!

My mother says this herself. Not about watch gears but about other things. She said it the time I washed my woolen sweater, the one Mamma had knitted, in hot water and it shrunk. I'd dropped chocolate pudding down the front of it and Mamma told me to rinse it quickly before it

49

stained. Out the window! She had shouted. A good sweater, out the window! But she said it in Yiddish—Aroyse gavorfen! and only translated when I shouted that I didn't know what she was saying. Schrei nisht! Miriam! My grandmother had shouted when my mother told her about it, which I did understand since my grandmother says this often and Leon has translated it. Don't yell! Shrei nisht! "All that good work, aroyse gavorfen! Out the window!" shouted Mamma.

Next I pick out the sardine can. It has some blue paint on it that looks like an eye. He'd like this too, I'm thinking about Pablo. Pablo Picasso—what a nice name, I'm thinking too. I'm thinking Pablo and I could be friends if he didn't live in France and if he wasn't so much older than me, as old as the people who sit on the benches on Eastern Parkway, in the sun, talking to each other in Yiddish, or playing Pinochle.

But Pablo isn't sitting in the sun with his white, halo hair. He's rummaging through the garbage dump looking for things that are just too interesting to throw away. Pablo's big, dark eyes are piercing. Junk? They seem to ask. Isn't it all the way you look at it?

The cookie tin of fat is on my shelf, where I left it yesterday. I open it up. It smells a little like the locker room in the boy's gym. A little like old, unwashed socks, like David Mendelsohn's, jammed and forgotten in his locker, the day we all got to see them when Mr. Spier wrapped them in tin foil like cheese and told David he had to take them home.

I wrap the fat in one of Georgie's old diapers, from the rag bag in the closet, and decide to do a little rearranging. I move the salt water taffy barrel. Inside are nine-hundred-and-seventy-three plastic charms that I've collected, so far, from the nickel machine where they fall into my hand in a rush when I turn the handle, shining gold and silver, and all the colors of the rainbow.

My marble collection is in a chalk box that Pappa brought home from night school. I move it to the second shelf. I shift my rubber band ball and the pink and blue, woolen horse rein I've been working on since first grade. It's big as a beach ball. I move the basket of dolls from all the countries Aunt Dorothy has visited, and my paper doll books, to the top shelf. I decide to unwrap Georgie's diaper to look at the fat again. The pieces look smaller and not as white as they looked at the butcher's. "Suet," I say quietly, thinking how very much like old sneakers the suet smells. Sneakers that have been left out in the rain then worn too soon.

I look out the window. I'm thinking I should put it out in the back yard, but it's dark, and I'd have to walk past my mother in the kitchen to get to the door. Where are you going? She'd ask. Oh, just to put out this fat which smells a little funny, that's all. Nothing to worry about. I rewrap the fat and plan to put it out in the morning on the way to school. I get a bag from the kitchen and leave the fat by the door of my room to remember. I put back my things-found-in-the-street collection and straighten the cigar boxes that hold my trading cards.

I take the rubber band ball off the shelf and bounce it. I've been working on it for three years. The more rubber bands I add the higher it bounces. Now it's as good as a new Spalding. I could use it for my science project, I think. The more rubber the higher the bounce. That's interesting. Maybe for every ten or fifteen rubber bands it bounces a few more inches. There's a principle here, I'm thinking. I could keep adding rubber bands and keep measuring how high the ball bounces. There are plenty of rubber bands in the street and usually a few in the junk drawer in the kitchen. And my father keeps the ones he brings home from school in his desk.

I could do research about rubber and write about it. The Power of Rubber, I imagine calling my science project. I could talk about all the rubber bands in the street and tell about where I found them. Troy Avenue, between Crown and Montgomery. Schenectady in front of Bender's Department Store, in the lobby of Donna's building after the mailman leaves. I could write about the ones my cousin Natalie gave me from her braces when I admired them. I could report that she complained they were too tight, that she swallowed them without meaning to when she chewed taffy. They didn't taste so bad, she said. But she could feel them as they made their way down to her stomach, which scared her a little, enough to tell her mother, my Aunt Ida. Aunt Ida told her she'd have to wait until her teeth were straight before she could eat taffy. Natalie said it happens with Jube Jubes too, though she's decided not to tell this to Aunt Ida. I could write these things since Natalie lives in the Bronx and there's no way for it to get back to my Aunt Ida. "That would be some interesting science project!" I'm telling my doll, Hannah.

I bounce the ball. I bounce it again. Who would believe the spring to these things? With the next bounce the rubber band ball hits the ceiling. I decide to seriously consider it for the science fair. Then someone's tapping at my door.

"What's banging in there?" calls my mother. I put the ball back on my shelf and open my door. Mamma pokes in her head. She makes a face and sniffs. "What's that smell?" she asks.

"I—I'm tidying my shelves," I tell her. Mamma looks

around, frowning. But it's evening and she's tired. She sniffs again. "It must be in the street," she says and sighs. When she closes my door I open the window to get some air circulating. I take my horse rein off the shelf and work on it for a while, catching the loops of yarn with a safety pin, slipping them off each of its four nails which Pappa hammered into a thread spool. I pull down the growing rope of wool and admire its length with satisfaction. The Power of Rubber, I'm thinking. The Rubber Story. Small Bands Make a Big Bounce. Bounce of the Mighty Bands. Strength In Numbers. Rubber Bands: A Journey From Floor to Ceiling. Hmm, I'm thinking, people could guess how many rubber bands make up my rubber band ball. But then I'd have to count them. I'd have to undo and redo it. That would take some time. Or I could make another one and keep track as I go. That would take time too, even if I could find enough rubber bands. Three years work in two weeks? I don't know. And I'd have to give prizes, but what? Rubber bands, I'm thinking. But who would want rubber bands for a prize except me?

Or maybe I could use the fat collection. Benny Pitt says the birds love fat. Suet, Dahling, suet! I can hear him say it. I could see which birds come to the back yard, then look them up in a bird book. I could draw pictures of them. The Birds of Crown Street. The Birds In My Back Yard. Or, Back Yard Birds. Birds and Fat. Now that's got an interesting sound!

Of course there is always my rock collection. I've been collecting and labeling rocks for two years. Sam, my future brother-in-law, once admired the piece of quartz crystal I got at the souvenir shop when my father took us to Howe Caverns. Sam is an engineer, a kind of scientist. Sam gave me a piece of mica, the window of an old lantern. He thought I could use it, he said, for "my impressive rock collection." Sam wants me to like him. Pappa says my rock collection is "very interesting," and he writes about science for the newspaper. Two scientists' opinions. Maybe, just maybe.

Tomorrow the third grade is going to the museum. I put down my horse rein and walk over to the dresser and the magazine. I'm startled into laughing by Pablo Picasso's dark eyes, as if he's here. Maybe I should use my things-found-in-the-street collection for the science fair, I'm thinking as I change into my pajamas. I think of his antelope sculpted out of found objects. Objects no one would have looked twice at. "No one but you and me," I whisper to Picasso's picture. I get down the coffee can and empty it out on my bed. I arrange the contents on my blanket. I look at the face in the can opener. What possibilities. "Found Objects." I say it quietly, loving the sound, thinking about the way they inspire Pablo Picasso and me. I put the pieces back into the can, and return the can to its place on the shelf. I pick up my horse rein again, wrap the pink and blue wool around a nail, slip off the loop with my safety pin, imagining the sculptures I could make. Wrapping the wool again, slipping it past the nail, wrapping it again. "Assemblage," I say out loud. "Assem-blaaage," like music. "You're an artist, Ruthie," I can hear my father saying, and again my eyes sting, and that funny tight feeling in my throat happens.

I put down my horse rein and pick up Hannah. "I really have to get serious about that collection," I tell her. Maybe start digging in the alley for more stuff that may be buried in the dirt, I think. Art Or Junk? I imagine as the title for a report for school. I'd read it to Pappa and Mamma. "Junk!" I imagine my mother answering.

I put my horse rein back on the shelf noticing how much longer it's grown while I've been thinking about

Picasso and me. Thinking takes time, I think, and wonder if there's a project there. "Time and Thought," I say out loud, then notice that my room is getting cool. I close my window. I can feel the warm air in eddies. Hmm, I think. The cool air is pushing the warm air! That's science too! "Weather," I tell Hannah. Science is everywhere, I'm thinking next. What a title that would make, but I can't write about all of it so I'm back to where I started.

Rocks, rubber bands, fat and Pablo Picasso's black eyes float through the dark as I lay awake staring at the ceiling. My head feels like a malted machine. I imagine myself walking through the gymnasium at school, panicky because I have no science project.

In the morning I remember I've been dreaming of going to my cousins' in Queens, riding in Pappa's car, passing the landfill on our way, all of us holding our noses. Even after my eyes are open I can still smell it. I lie there thinking of my dream. "Roll up the windows," I can hear Pappa say. I like to watch the seagulls dive at that big loaf of garbage but the smell makes Rebecca wretch. Then I notice it's my room that smells--just like the landfill.

Oh my God, it's the fat! I have to put it outside! I have to remember! I pull open the window. Suet, suet, suet, I tell myself as I get dressed. Suet, as I pull on my sweater and socks, suet suet suet suet as I kiss Hannah and grab my school bag. I switch Hannah from the high chair to her crib, thinking she'll nap until I get home. Where's my key? What was I just thinking? There's a sensation at the back of my nose as I rummage through my top drawer until I find it, strung on its satin ribbon. I'm dimly aware the sensation is relieved as I close the door of my room and walk up the hall to the kitchen.

"There will be things at the museum that may give you good ideas for your science projects," Mrs. Roth tells us before we leave our room to get onto the bus. We file through the hall past closed classroom doors. My stomach feels like clouds at the thought of leaving the school building to take a trip. Fast blowing clouds on a windy, beautiful day. "It's like a holiday," says Donna. "It's like a jailbreak," says David Mendelsohn.

We pass the boys' locker room. That's when I remember that I forgot to put out the suet.

The Museum

At the museum we wander through the dinosaurs, the marine animals and the Hall of Indigenous Peoples. Then, suddenly, we're in the middle of the gem and mineral collection, rows and rows of glass cases with rocks from all over the world. I begin to feel light-headed. There's this feeling in the pit of my stomach—a wanting, collecting feeling, an imagining-these-rocks-on-my-shelf feeling. Lavender amethyst, yellow citron, pink, blue and rust colored quartz crystal, big chunks of them. A sea of rocks! I whisper, then look self consciously around. I imagine them sitting neatly on my shelf while I'm at school, waiting quietly for me to look at and count when I get home. They'd sit next to the carton of rocks I've found in the back yard. But there isn't any more room on that shelf. I imagine stacking them on top of the shelves. Only a few would fit. I might have to ask Pappa to build another shelf, maybe another few shelves. More than a few, I'm thinking, and a bigger room, a few of them, or a house, a gem and minerals house, a museum of my own, really. That's what I'm imagining, my heart beating fast as we

56

shuffle along behind Mrs. Roth, past the cases of geodes, rocks that look ordinary on the outside but inside look like something from another world. The place looks like an electric rainbow, I'm saying to myself. Where do you find these things?

"Hurry or we'll get behind!" Donna calls. But I can't read the labels that fast, lined up in neat rows with all their N's. My eyes feel stuck to the glass cases with those sparkling chunks of magic inside. "Ruthie!" says Donna, suddenly beside me, pulling my arm.

"Everyone is in the fossil room!" "I can't believe this stuff!" I tell Donna. "It would take days to get through this place and see every rock and read every label!"

I've begun to imagine living in the gem and mineral room, not for that long, say a weekend, or maybe a few months, just until I could see everything. I could pitch a tent, bring a cot or a sleeping bag, say, like camping. I imagine getting up at night and wandering around just taking in all those colors. My parents would miss me, and I'd miss them, but we could visit and I wouldn't have to listen to Rebecca call me stupid, or to Georgie's crying. Pappa, could you build me a room? I'd ask, just something small—at first. Then I realize Donna is pushing me from behind. "You look like a zombie!" she's saying.

The next room has the same kind of lit glass cases, full of rows and rows of fossils. Petrified wood and petrified bugs. Rocks with impressions of snails and fish and leaves and clam shells, sitting in perfect, petrified rows. And trilobites, things that are in the encyclopedia, ancient beetles looking like armored tanks. I imagine lining up the rocks that are jumbled in the carton on my shelf. I'd glue them onto paper. I could label them like the ones in the cases. But if I use them for the Science Fair I'll have to leave spaces for the N's if I use Pappa's old typewriter to make labels, then fill them in later with a pen. Or maybe I could hand write the labels entirely. Maybe I could actually find a geode. But where? In the back yard? Are there geodes in Brooklyn? Are there fossils? There must be! There must be fossils all over the world! I'm thinking. And Brooklyn is part of the world! I forget about everything, even Aylene Muntzer, looking at those rows and rows and rows of petrification.

Then we enter a room with a sign that reads, "Minerals Common to New York State." Inside these cases are pieces of granite and feldspar, mica schist, garnet crystals and conglomerate. A tiny piece of garnet has broken off and is lying by itself. I imagine lifting the glass top and rescuing it, bringing it home, gluing it down, welcoming it into my collection. I can use my father's shirt cardboards from Young's Laundry, I'm thinking. Much better than plain paper. "Garnet Crystal," I'd type, hand writing the n. Perfect, I'm imagining.

A chorus is singing in the pit of my stomach—rocks, rocks, rocks, it's singing. Rocks, labeled and spelled right. And I don't at first realize that I'm the only one left in the Minerals Common To New York State room except for a man and woman I've never seen before. Just the three of us in this huge room. It's like waking up from a dream of another world, bright with rainbows of colors. Rock colors! The man and woman are looking into the cases.

A sleeping bag in a room as big and empty as the grand canyon? I'm suddenly asking myself, picturing it at night with the lights off. I begin to hurry through rows of cases into the hall of stuffed animals, past stuffed beavers and mice, armadillos, gazelles, aardvarks, zebras, then the elephants in the dioramas of Africa, dimly wondering why they kill animals to stuff. Then I'm in a room of stuffed birds, then butterflies pinned to the wall and still, not like the ones that flutter in the back yard. Not like the ones knocking around in my stomach, making it feel kind of sick. Where's Mrs. Roth? Where's Donna? Where's my class? What if they leave without me?

Now my heart is pounding. How will I get home? How will I get out of this museum? The rooms go on forever. Ancient pottery, Greek urns, African masks, fish, whales. What if they close the museum with me in it? Hardly anyone comes here, just our class and that man and woman, I'm thinking, racing past the sign, "Life Beneath The Earth's Surface," past dried wasps and rabbit warrens under glass, thinking, I'll never see my brother Georgie again, never hear him cry, never see my parents or Rebecca or Leon.

My eyes are stinging, tears coming up to their edges like magnifying glasses making the marble walls and floor look curved and floating. Then the tears spill over.

I hear a door creak open as I race through the Sea Mammals. I turn. Next to the giant squid a museum guard pokes in his head. "Are you Ruthie Pincus?" he asks. I wipe my eyes. "Yes—" I answer. Another guard looks in through a door between the jelly fish and eels. "Did you find her?" he asks. "She's right here!" answers the first guard. "I'll call upstairs," he says. He smiles. "You scared your teacher," he tells me. "Come on, your class is in the souvenir shop."

Mrs. Roth looks relieved. I thought I'd have to stay here, I want to cry. I thought I'd never see my family again, and I wonder why she's suddenly bending toward me, frowning and pale, and why her hand on my shoulder feels so heavy. Then she hugs me, rummages in her pocket book, presses a tissue into my hand. "You can take out your souvenir money," she calls, and then she's moving away. My cheeks are burning and I'm swallowing shudders that keep coming up from my stomach which is wobbling like jelly. "Where were you?" says Donna into my ear. Then she sees my face. Her pupils dilate so wide that the circles of her eyes look black with a thin rim of blue as she leans toward me, frowning too. Then her mouth twists in sympathy and she takes my hand. Tears start dropping onto my blouse and I hiccup. I remember the tissue and hold it to my eyes. "Wanna go rock hunting after school?" she asks. I nod and put my head down.

The rest of the class is buying souvenirs. Evy Mailman is buying a pencil with a bear eraser. David Mendelsohn is buying a plastic squid, shaking the tentacles at Marty Bush. Aylene is buying a shell fossil. It costs five dollars. Aylene Muntzer always has more money than anyone else.

There are sets of rocks and minerals for sale for three dollars. They have crystals and little geodes. One has mica schist, and a piece of pyrite, fool's gold. Aylene buys that too. "Why is it called 'fool's gold?'" Davine is asking Mrs. Roth. Mrs. Roth tells Davine that in the days of the California Gold Rush people thought it was the real thing. Davine says she thinks it's prettier than gold. "So who are the fools?" David Mendelsohn, who's standing next to Davine, asks our teacher. Aylene looks annoyed. Mrs. Roth looks like she'd like to go home.

The rows of rocks and minerals in black paper covered boxes are neatly labeled miniatures of the rocks in the display cases. My heart beats in my ears just looking at them. Three dollars. I take out the dollar that's left in my pocket after having given Mrs. Roth seventy-five cents for lunch and the bus. I look at it and put it back in my pocket. If I save it and add this week's milk money and my allowance I can buy it next week. Then I remember

Hannah's carriage set at Bender's Department Store which still has to be paid for. But maybe Mamma will let me iron Pappa's shirts and handkerchiefs, maybe even sheets and pillow cases. Somehow I can't imagine my mother paying me to iron pillow cases and sheets which she doesn't iron herself. But wouldn't they look nicer smooth? I could ask her. Wouldn't they look like sheets in a magazine? Wouldn't they smell good? I could say. And I imagine my mother's face. She'd frown like Mrs. Roth. Then I'm thinking how thirsty I'll be without milk. There's the water fountain in the hall outside our classroom. It spouts warm water.

Donna buys a whistle shaped like a horse. "Aren't you going to buy a souvenir?" she asks. I shake my head. Donna's mouth twists up again.

When I get home I tell Mamma about the gem and mineral room and the sets in the souvenir shop. I ask if she or Pappa or maybe Leon could take me back there in a few weeks, on, say, a Saturday.

"Is that all you think I have to do?" she asks sharply. I look at her. She's rubbing the toe of her stocking with a bar of soap, rinsing it in a basin in the sink. She glances at me. Her eyes look funny. Her face looks pinched. In his room Georgie starts complaining. My brother Georgie doesn't like it when anyone but Georgie talks to Mamma. But Mamma doesn't hurry down the hall to Georgie's room. "With a back yard full of rocks we don't need to pay good money to buy them!" she says. She doesn't look at me softly then, as she usually does after her voice is hard. "Saturdays—" says my mother picking up the other stocking, "Saturdays I'm going to visit Aunt Rose."

"Saturdays?" I repeat, thinking she must have meant to say "Saturday." My mother doesn't answer. She runs

61

the water over her stocking, letting the other lie in the sink. It drifts with the water's motion, looking like a caught fish. I wait. "The museum is open Sundays, could we go then?" "No!" answers Mamma. "I'll be tired. Don't question me." I look hard at her until she turns to me again. First she pinches her mouth shut, rolling in her lips until they're just a line. "Aunt Rose," my mother says. "Aunt Rose isn't—well, Ruthie." She presses her mouth closed and looks into the sink. I hear the buzz of the refrigerator and it sounds too loud.

"When will she get better?" I ask. "Mamma—?" My stomach feels like the rocks from the museum are inside it.

"I don't know," my mother says quietly. "She's in a hospital—upstate. Pappa and I will go—on Saturdays. Aunt Dorothy and Grandma Anna will visit during the week."

Georgie is sobbing at the door of his room. I can see him from where Mamma and I are standing. Mamma would see him too if she turned her head, but she doesn't. But Georgie can see us. He throws himself onto the floor and starts screaming. My mother is just looking into the basin, letting the water run. Then I watch it drip, thinking she's turned off the tap and realize the drops are Mamma's tears. My stomach feels so full of rocks I feel weighed down. Like I might fall. "Wait, Georgie!" I call down the hall. "Mamma, what sickness is it?" I ask. Mamma turns and puts her finger to her lips. "It's a—" then she's holding her hand over her mouth. I lean toward the sink and turn off the water. With almost no sound she says, "—a mental illness—."

"MAA-MAA!" my brother is shrieking. My father's key turns in the door. He looks down the hall at Georgie, turns toward us, then walks down the hall. "Oh, Georgie," says Pappa, trying to pick my brother up. Georgie is screaming, slamming his feet against the floor. Pappa comes back to the kitchen. "Miriam?" he's asking. Now Mamma is crying into her handkerchief. Pappa moves in her direction but she waves him away. "Take Georgie into his room, David," she says. The words are muffled through her handkerchief. My father looks at me, his brow shadowing his eyes. He walks back down the hall to Georgie. "Come on, Georgie," my father coaxes. "Come, son, bubela, come." Then Georgie's sobs and my father's soft voice are muted by the closed door.

Mamma blows her nose and looks at me. Her eyes are dark and still. She hugs me. "Ruthie, you're a comfort to me," she tells me. My arms hold her, they won't let her go. She sniffs and blows her nose again over my shoulder.

I do my math homework, trying to stop the numbers from swimming all over my notebook page. Mental illness, mental illness, I can't get the words out of my head, or the image of my mother's stocking rippling in the sink, her tears dropping like rain into the basin. I think of my Aunt Rose. I can see her, looking beautiful, in her bright pink wool coat and red lipstick, her sleek black hair pulled back behind her ears. The coat is long, with a long pink belt, the belt I learned to tie a knot on. I remember her face when I looked up at her, think of her smile that lit up the kitchen that winter night. Then I'm thinking about the Indian Nuts she bought my sister and me, once, from the nickel machine. And I'm thinking of the way she calls us Becky and Rudy, names no one else calls us but Aunt Rose. "Rose is the most beautiful of the three of us," I can hear Aunt Dorothy say.

Going back to the museum doesn't seem important

now.

Rock Hunting

This is New York State, I'm thinking. What if I find some hornblende, or feldspar, or a garnet crystal like the one in the glass case at the museum? What if I find a fossil? Pappa's shirt cardboards will be perfect to glue them onto and label them like the sets at the museum. A perfect project, I think, for the Science Fair.

I knock softly at the door of my father's study and turn the knob. My father stops typing and looks up. His hair is ruffled. His eyes are there but I know he doesn't see me. He's seeing the article he's writing. He's working on a deadline.

I wait. Slowly Pappa's eyes focus and he smiles. "Can I use the hammer?" I ask. "The hammer?" says Pappa. I nod. I'm not really sure he's heard me even though he's spoken. He's thinking of Einstein or stars or weather patterns, maybe sea life—he's thinking of the thing he's writing about for his science article.

"The hammer," I repeat. "Can I use it, Pappa? I'm going rock hunting." I wait. Pappa looks down at his article. So I speak slowly and with emphasis. "Pappa—I—need—it—for—the SCIENCE FAIR," I say. My father raises his head. He looks straight at me.

"The Science Fair?" he repeats.

"Pappa! You should see the rocks at the museum! I need the hammer, Pappa, to find some of my own in the alley! Rocks! Maybe a geode or a fossil, for the SCIENCE FAIR! Donna and I are going rock hunting!"

My father takes off his glasses and runs his hand through his hair. "Do you know how to open rocks?" he asks looking confused.

I nod, vigorously. "With a hammer, Pappa!" I answer.

64

He really looks at me now. Then he tells me he's worried about my eyes.

In all the photos of my father as a child he's wearing glasses. Besides calling me "doll" and "sugar" my father calls me "sharp eyes." He says it when I read road signs he isn't able to see. Take care of them, Sugar, he says, switching on the lamp when I read, they have to last a lifetime! He tells my sister, Rebecca, the same thing. And my brother, Leon. "Pappa, I know, my eyes," Leon reassures him before he leaves for football practice. "I'll pull down my face mask."

"Pappa, I'll be careful," I tell him now, hoping the furrows will soften in his forehead. My father gets up. He goes down to the basement. I can hear him rummaging. He comes back upstairs, stops at the hall closet. When he reappears at the door of his study he's holding the hammer, a pair of goggles and an old pink towel.

"Goggles, Pappa?"

My father frowns. "Ruthie, please. One pair, that's all anyone gets."

I nod. Pappa smiles. "Wrap them in the towel," he's saying. "Then hit it—hard!"

"And watch your fingers!" he calls as I shut the door.

I walk to the corner apartment building and ring the bell that says Pukatch and watch Donna jog down the marble lobby stairs, the fringe on her cowgirl jacket swinging. Donna Pukatch is my best friend. She's carrying a folded paper bag for her rocks.

The alley stretches behind the row of two-family houses and the apartment buildings that line Crown Street between Troy and Schenectady Avenues. Here clotheslines that hang across back yards are fastened to garages and telephone poles. Garbage cans are lined up, and steel barrels of burned coal. And here is kept the Solloway's big German Shepherd, Captain. Captain sits behind the Solloway's hurricane fence, behind a sign that reads "Keep Out."

Captain's yellow eyes take in Donna, then me. He snorts.

On the other side of the alley are the back yards of Montgomery Street. The alley is like a border between two countries, Crown and Montgomery. Kids from Crown and Montgomery look at each other, and sometimes even talk, over the fences that delineate our territories. Even though we all see each other at school.

It's where I first saw Davine Hoffman's cousin, Jessie, who lives on Montgomery Street, and Davine, standing right next to him. It surprised me to see someone I knew, as if Davine were standing in another world. The alley is where the older kids play tag and Ringalivio—older kids from both streets. Now it's deserted and quiet, except for Captain, who is snarling in our direction.

"Maybe this one's a geode," says Donna, scratching at a stone lodged in the sand between the asphalt and Mr. Solloway's grass. I dig it out with the hammer's prongs. I take the towel from my paper bag, wrap the rock and lay it on the broken asphalt. This upsets Captain. His snarls become higher pitched as he strains against his collar chain, his lip is raised, showing his teeth. He's drooling like he'd like to have Donna and me for lunch. I look from Donna to Captain. Now he's straining so hard against his chain that his voice disappears altogether and he's gasping.

Donna tries talking to him. "Good boy, it's okay—" she tells him in a friendly voice. "He's going to choke himself, poor thing." She puts out her hand in his direction and

Captain lunges. "Let's go down near my house," says Donna. I pick up the rock, flash my teeth at Captain and agree. Captain goes crazy, squealing and hurling himself against his chain. The Solloway's window opens. Mrs. Solloway's head pokes out. She glares at us. Donna picks up the hammer and towel and pulls me by the arm. We walk four houses down until we're behind Donna's apartment building.

I put the pink terry cloth package down on the asphalt again. Oh, please be a geode, I'm thinking, or something I can use for my rock collection, something other than the mostly white quartz that now sits on my shelf. I put on my goggles. Donna looks at me. "Where did you get those?" she asks. "My father," I answer. "In case the rock splinters. Better stand back and shut your eyes," I tell Donna. Donna nods. Donna wears glasses. I lift the hammer, squeeze my eyes shut and smack the bundle with all my strength. The sound makes Captain bark. We peel back the towel. Then I'm thinking I'm seeing blue, green, yellow crystals until I realize they're just blotches in the air from holding my breath and squeezing my eyelids shut.

"Look at all those pieces!" says Donna. Her voice is almost drowned out by Captain's barking. "They're white," I say. Donna nods. "White quartz," I say and frown. "That's good, isn't it?" asks Donna. I shrug. "I already have a whole collection of it," I tell her. "Good you wrapped it," she says. "It would have flown all over the place." I nod. Captain's fallen quiet. "We only have one pair of eyes—" I tell Donna. "But there's plenty of white quartz," I say looking over at Captain, who, when he sees my gaze shift to him starts barking again. "You sound like Mrs. Roth," calls Donna. "My father!" I answer. "Tell Aylene," says Donna, biting the nail on her pinky. "When she calls me Four Eyes." Donna's looking at me. I twist my mouth in sympathy.

"Try calling her peasant," I suggest. "That's what my father tells me to call Rebecca when she calls me Flat Face."

"A peasant is a farmer," says Donna.

"Farmers are good," I agree. "Better just call her a jerk." Donna shrugs. I shrug back.

"Still," she says, "it could have been a geode."

We're twisting our mouths. "Maybe I'll start a collection of white quartz. I'll label them, white quartz, white quartz, white quartz—" Donna and I start laughing. Captain loses it. His yelps echo off the walls of the buildings that line the alley. Mrs. Solloway's window opens again. "Ruthie Pincus, stop that racket!" she's calling. "White Quartz of Brooklyn," I'm struggling to say between spasms of laughter. "What is your science project?" asks Donna, trying to sound like Mrs. Roth. "A Lot of White Quartz," I answer. The alley is quiet and I realize Captain's stopped barking. "Maybe he's getting tired," says Donna. "Maybe laughter confuses him," I say. "They do look interesting," says Donna about the fragments of white quartz. "I'll be relieved when the Science Fair is over," I say. We divide the pieces and put them in our bags. We take our things and start home.

"Ruthie Pincus takes first prize for her White Quartz Collection," says Donna as we come up to Captain. "Three Hundred Pieces of Quartz All Shapes And Sizes," I say. "White," adds Donna. "Very unusual," she says, sounding like our teacher. Then we're laughing again, trying to catch our breath. Captain remembers his voice. "White Quartz for everyone!" I shout to Captain. This causes him to lurch against his collar again and his voice rises to a scream. The window squeals open and Mrs. Solloway shouts that she's going to tell our mothers. We lower our heads and hurry toward the gate to my back yard. At least white quartz doesn't have any N's, I'm thinking.

The next day we try again, smashing stones in the alley behind Donna's apartment building, taking turns wearing the goggles while Captain snarls, his chain ringing against the Solloway's metal fence. With every rock we smash he goes crazy. "All white quartz," I say to Donna. Then it's her turn. "Hey, this one's pink!" she declares, peeling back the towel. Tiny red crystals sparkle in the sunlight. "It's granite!" I tell her. I recognize it from the museum. "What are those red things?" says Donna. "They're—garnet!" I whisper in awe. "Like the ones in the museum?" Donna whispers back. I nod, my eyes fastened to the glittering particles of red. Then we fall silent as if we were seeing someone famous walking down Crown Street, a famous rock, famous enough to get into the Natural History Museum. Even Aylene's set doesn't have garnet crystals.

We find a piece of black granite, more white quartz and an old brick. "Do you think this would count as a rock?" I ask Donna. Donna just looks at me. I smash it open anyway and find a shell. "I didn't know bricks were made with shells," says Donna.

"That's worthy of a science project." I look at the shell's impression in the brick's red clay. "It's like a fossil," I say. "Just man made. I can say that on a label." Donna nods. "It's got an n," she says. She knows about Pappa's typewriter. I nod and frown. I put the brick into my bag.

We hunt for rocks until it's too dark to see and I remember that I still have to finish my math homework. "Want some white quartz?" I ask Donna. "Do you mind if I start a rock collection?" she

asks. "We could both become archeologists!" I answer. We smile.
We divvy up the white quartz and the fragments of pink granite
with its bits of garnet. Then we linger in the quiet evening talking
for a while, about still being best friends even when we are grown
ups, and archeologists.

We listen to the halting squeal of a pulley, as someone
reels in their dried laundry.

"My Aunt Rose is in the hospital," I say softly.

Donna looks at me. "What's wrong with her?"

I press my lips together and shrug.

Donna twists up her mouth.

Captain has settled down. He looks at me as I pass.
He manages a snort. By the time I walk through my back
yard the moon is rising above the roof of our house. I slip
in through the side door.

My mother is furious. "Did you forget you have a
home?" she asks, glowering at me. "It's after dark, I was
about to call the Pukatches when Mrs. Solloway called!
Next I would have called the police!" She eyes my paper
bag.

I look at Mamma and take a breath. "Donna and I
went rock hunting," I tell her. "For my new—collection."

Mamma's eyes narrow. They look through me.
"Mamma, maybe I'll use it for my science project—I'm
deciding."

My mother sighs. She looks into the bag. "They're full
of dirt!" she says.

"Mamma—I'll wash them," I tell her.

"Mamma!" My little brother, Georgie, calls from the
bathroom.

Then comes Rebecca's voice: "Mamma, Georgie won't
let me take him out of the bath tub!"

"MAA-MAA!" Georgie shouts. "I WANT TO GET OUT!"

"Come, Georgie!" I hear Rebecca say. "Mamma, he wants you!" she calls.

"MAMMA, THERE'S A TURTLE IN HERE!" yells my brother.

"A wha—aat?" answers Mamma, turning, starting for the bathroom. "And swordfiiiiish!" Mammaaaa, get me out of HEEEE-RRRE! AND SHARKS, MAAMAAAA! GET ME OUTTT!" When my mother turns back she looks tired and worried. "Wash up, Ruthie, and set the table for supper. "Wait, Georgie, I'm coming!" she calls hurrying down the hall to the bathroom.

I close the door to my room. I move things around on my collection shelf to make space for my rocks. I stand the cigar boxes on their sides. That makes room for the salt water taffy barrel of plastic charms. I stack the dog pictures album on top of my paper doll collection which leaves half of the middle shelf clear. I step back and look with satisfaction at the empty space waiting for my rocks. I imagine them stacked neatly with shirt cardboards, glued with stones from the alley. I'll scotch tape the cardboard to make trays. I look at the shelf again. There's room for ten trays if I can find enough interesting rocks to fill them. Maybe I'll just wash a few, just very quickly, I'm thinking. I look into the bag. The bottom is full of dirt and bits of asphalt. Mamma and Georgie are still in the bathroom. I could use the hose in the back yard but there isn't time before supper and I have to set the table. I decide to use the pail and fill it with water from the kitchen sink. I get the pail from the broom closet and hurry to the kitchen, fill it with water and haul it to my room. It drips onto my floor. I need a towel, but Georgie

71

and Mamma are still in the bathroom. There's the rag bag in the hall closet but I should be setting the table. I grab for my pajamas folded under my pillow, put them on the floor and set down the pail. I empty the bag of stones into the water. Wet dirt and asphalt splash onto my pajamas.

I hear Mamma and Georgie leave the bathroom. I'll set the table then carry the pail into the bathroom, I'm thinking, to wash the stones one by one. As soon as they dry I'll start gluing. I take one last satisfied look at the waiting space on my shelf when I notice something seems different about the one underneath. Something is missing.

Rancid

Between my horse rein and my marbles, there's a gap that looks like a lost tooth. What was there? I'm trying to remember.

I count my dolls—eleven, right. Two trading card boxes—right. My rock collection, yes. Wait. It's not a tooth, it's my fat collection. It was next to my trading cards. Then I remember the way it smelled. And I remember that I put it near the door of my room so that I wouldn't forget to put it outside in the back yard. And, I'm thinking, my room smells normal now.

I walk up the hall to the kitchen.

"Why isn't the table set?" says my mother.

"My fat collection is missing," I answer.

Mamma is seasoning meat in the broiler. She turns off the stove, leaves the broiler open. Her eyes meet mine. There's a look on her face." Ruthie, listen..." Her mouth stays open, one of her eyebrows is up, one is down.

"It was in my room, Mamma—I meant to put it outside..."

"Ruthie, it smelled, darling. Your sister found it next

72

to the door. The smell was in the hallway!"

My cheeks begin to warm. "I was going to put it out—for the birds, Mamma," I say. My mother is looking at me. "It smelled," she repeats. "The hallway smelled!"

It made your sister feel sick!" And now her voice is rising. "The whole house SMELLED!"

Now I can't keep words in and I'm yelling too. "But where did you PUT IT? It was going to be my SCIENCE PROJECT! Maybe."

"WHAT IS THE MATTER WITH YOU? IT WAS FAT! JUST FAT!" hollers my mother.

"WAS? WAS? WAS?!" I holler back. I hear my father's door open. I feel tears spill over the edges of my eyes, sliding down my cheeks to my neck, then inside my sweater to my chest.

"Ruthie, you can't collect meat on a shelf in your room," says my mother in a quieter voice. "It has to be refrigerated!"

"It wasn't meat!" I tell my mother. "It was FAT! Beautiful, white FAT! Fat the birds would have eaten! Benny Pitt gave it to me for the BIRDS!"

"Ruthie—" says Mamma, moving close to me. She puts out her hand to touch my shoulder. I step back so she can't reach me.

I see my father through thick lenses of tears as he appears at the kitchen doorway from the hall. "Sugar—" says my father. I can barely see him but his voice is gentle and I can see his eyebrows are pulled down at their outsides. "Miriam—" he says to my mother.

My mother takes off her apron, leaves it on the chair, walks down the hall to my parents' bedroom and closes the door.

"It looked too nice to just throw it away," I'm gulping,

telling my father. My face is soaking and my nose is running. My father wipes my face with his handkerchief and puts his arms around me. "Benny Pitt said the birds would like it!" I'm crying into his sweater. The words come in blobs like blobs of whitefish and carp out of my grandmother's meat grinder when she makes gefilte fish. "I was going to—blob—blob, put it—blob—in the back yard—blob—for the them—but I forgot." My father strokes my hair. He lifts my chin with his fingers. He smiles. "Pappa it wasn't just fat, it was—a—science project!" I'm telling my father, sniffing, trying to pull air through my nose but it's packed and I have to breathe through my mouth. "Set the table, Ruthie," says Pappa. "Blow your nose, Sweetheart" he says, handing me his handkerchief. He kisses me and walks down the hall, then knocks softly at the door of my parents' bedroom.

I eat supper but don't listen to what anyone is saying at the table. My sister doesn't look at me when Mamma tells her to pass me the gravy.

"Give it to your sister," she also says about the extra peaches in syrup for dessert. Then I glare at Rebecca and she looks away, holding the dish of peaches until Pappa has to take it from her hands.

BOOK THREE

Salami

I'm sitting at the table pasting dog pictures I've collected in the loose leaf binder labeled "Dogs." Mamma is cutting up vegetables for soup. Georgie is standing on a chair at the sink washing potatoes and carrots. My mother has left an onion on the sink drainer. Georgie leans over to inspect it.

My brother Georgie likes to smell things. Pappa says it's the way he understands the world. He also likes to lick things, which makes my mother crazy. "Georgie, it's full of germs!" Mamma exclaims. "What are germs?" asks Georgie. "They're things that make you sick!" cries Mamma. "But I don't see anything!" says my brother. "Georgie," says Mamma. "It's dirty!" Though Georgie doesn't ever seem to mind dirt, he can understand this concept. Now, suddenly, my brother, Georgie, starts screaming. "I'm CRYING!" he's screaming. "MAMMA, I'M CRYING!"

I hear Leon's door open. "This is news?" Leon says into the hall.

"What's the matter?" my father calls from his study.

"Georgie is dying," says my sister, Rebecca from her room.

"Rebecca!" Pappa calls sternly.

"Let go of that onion!" Mamma is pleading with my little brother. "Georgie!" she finally screams. "Drop it!" "I'm crying, Mamma," Georgie is whimpering. "Georgie, it's from the onion," my mother is explaining.

I'm moving around dog pictures and wondering how I'll make good on my promise to my doll, Hannah, to bring

75

her something from the nickel toy machine. She's only a doll, I know, and my sister, Rebecca never gets tired of telling me this while slumping her shoulders and shaking her head. But it isn't quite true. Not to me. Hannah is a person, as far as I see it. And a promise is a promise.

"Oi!" declares my mother suddenly. "Ruthie, run back to the butcher's, we left the bag of feet! Hurry—I'll have to use the pressure cooker for the soup or we won't eat until midnight."

"What a shame," says Mamma to herself, using the Yiddish—a shanda! "My mother never used a pressure cooker to make soup!" she adds.

I hurry past the cleaners. Next is Kogen's. My steps slow. One of the Kogen brothers is building a stack of cough syrup boxes in the window. He's watching a box jiggle then stop as it finds its balance. He smiles at the box. I wish I could stay to watch. Suddenly his eyes catch mine and he looks startled. I wave. It's Abe.

The bells on Benny Pitt's door jingle. Benny Pitt looks up and smiles. He's on the telephone. "A little later I'll deliver it, Dahling," he's saying. "Moshe just went out—no? Hmm? M-hmm? You need the pot roast meat right away? All right, let me see, Dahling, hmm." The butcher smiles at me. "Ah, Ruthie!" he whispers, nodding, holding out the bag of chicken feet. "Thank you," I whisper, nodding back.

"Okay, Dahling," he says into the telephone. "I'll find someone right away—heh? Yes, in time to cook your dinner, don't worry."

Benny Pitt hangs up the telephone. I turn the knob of the door, look over my shoulder and wave goodbye. The bells on the door jingle. The butcher's hands are on his hips. He's looking at me. He lifts his hand to wave. "The pot roast, the pot roast—" he's murmuring. Suddenly his waving hand reaches toward me. "Ruthie!" he calls. "Wait, Dahling—could you do me a favor?"

I step back inside the butcher shop and let the door close. I look at Benny Pitt. "Mrs. Berman—" he says. "She needs to make her supper. Bring to her the meat, yes?"

"But—Mamma's soup..." I say.

"Dahling, it's around the corner, it will take a minute," he tells me. "It's for her supper, Mrs. Berman has no one to send—" He's looking at me, waiting. "I'll have to hurry," I hear myself say. "Thanks, Dahling!" says Benny Pitt. "Here, leave the feet. You'll get them when you come back with the money." He scribbles the name 'Berman' on the bag with the pot roast meat. "One, eight, seven—" says the butcher. "A dollar eighty-seven cents, Mrs. Berman will give you. Thank you, Ruthie!" he says as he dials Mrs. Berman on the telephone. "Ruthie Pincus is coming right away with the meat," he tells her. "Ruthie who? Ruthie Pincus, Miriam Pincus' daughter—you'll have it for supper—two minutes, Dahling!"

Mrs. Berman and her miniature poodle, Shatsie, live on the fourth floor of the apartment house on the corner of Crown Street and Troy Avenue, on the other side of the street from Donna Pukatch, across the hall from Joannie Nevins. I hurry back past Kogen's and the cleaners, turn the corner and take the wide, painted red concrete steps two at a time. Then I'm crossing the courtyard of the apartment building. I push against the heavy glass door with its iron flowered grate that opens into the vestibule, rows and rows of apartment bells, and a second door. This door is locked. I ring the bell that reads "Berman—apartment 16." The sound of static and Shatsie barking blares suddenly from the holes in the brass plate on the wall. "Who's there?" asks Mrs. Berman faintly. "Shah! I can't hear!" she crackles to Shatsie. "Who? Crackle-crackle—who? Who—crackle crackle?"

"Uh—meat delivery!" I answer.

"Ruthie—crackle—Pincus—crackle—is that you?"

"Hi, Mrs. Berman," I call into the brass plate.

"One—crackle—minute!" says Mrs. Berman. The buzzer rings and I push against the door to the lobby. It opens with a loud screech that rings off the marble walls and floor. I take the lobby stairs down to the elevator. I press the elevator button. Cables groan into motion on the other side of the wall. Soon the lighted window of the elevator appears. I open the door, step inside and press four. The elevator sits there. Then, suddenly, the door lurches shut, shaking the elevator car and it begins to creep up the shaft. I think of my mother waiting for the chicken feet and the chicken feet waiting on Benny Pitt's counter.

The elevator's cables knock and bump. The car hums as it climbs. Bricks crawl past the window, then the number two, then slow bricks then three, then more bricks. I'm swallowing down the thought of it stopping at those bricks, of having to wait for someone to come and rescue me, the elevator light buzzing like a trapped hornet. I'm squeezing back the picture of no one coming, wondering if I could go to sleep and just forget about it, wondering if I'd starve. I've never tried to eat pot roast raw. I'm hoping Mrs. Berman would call Benny Pitt when I didn't show up and that Benny Pitt would call my parents. But then what? How would my parents start the elevator and get me out of here? My heart is moving up into my throat and my head feels light when the elevator stops at the fourth floor. I wait for the door to open. The light sounds like a diving airplane. I'm shuddering and can't stop, then realize it's not me but the elevator. The door lurches open and I let out my breath. I decide to walk down.

Shatsie is barking before I ring the bell. Mrs. Berman's brown eye peers at me through the peephole. "Who's there?" she asks.

"Uh—meat delivery," I answer, looking into Mrs. Berman's black pupil. The door opens as far as the chain. The smell of onions frying drifts into the hall. Shatsie is jumping, her nails skidding on Mrs. Berman's white linoleum. Mrs. Berman looks from my head to my shoes and back. I smile, trying to look friendly. The door closes and I hear the chain slide. She reappears, struggling to hold onto Shatsie, to keep her from running out into the hall. "Shatsie! Wait! Wait! Shatsie!" Mrs. Berman is saying. She's bent over, holding Shatsie by the collar with one hand, reaching up for the bag of pot roast meat with the other. I hand it to her. "Wait! Wait!" she repeats, this time looking at me. She slams the door shut. When it opens she's wearing her glasses. She's holding Shatsie and her purse. Shatsie is wild, licking her face, barking at me, squealing, struggling to get out of Mrs. Berman's arms. Mrs. Berman is struggling to count out a dollar eighty seven, using one hand. "Here, Ruthie," she finally says breathlessly, handing me the money. "Say hello to your Mamma for me!"

"I wi—" I begin, but the door slams closed before I can finish. "Shatsie!" Mrs. Berman is calling on the other side of the door. "Shatsie, sit! SIT!"

I shiver as I pass the elevator and head for the stairs. Joannie Nevins' door opens and my heart drops. Joannie Nevins is the last person I want to meet. But it's only Joannie's mother and Joannie's little sister, Rachel, in the stroller.

"Hi, Mrs. Nevins," I say.

"Ruthie, could you hold the elevator door?" asks Mrs. Nevins. She tilts the carriage so the wheels will clear the gap between the elevator car and the edge of the fourth floor. If you look down that space I know you can see the bottom of the elevator shaft below the basement. A bolt like lightning shoots from my stomach to my knees. I keep my eyes up. I turn and smile at Mrs. Nevins, holding her eyes. Then, trying not to bend my head, I look at the green wool blanket, like the yellow one in Bender's window, tucked around Rachel. "What a very nice blanket," I say. "Thanks, Ruthie!" Mrs. Nevins says, smiling too. I hold the door and push the back of the carriage until it's in the elevator. Then I just stand there my eyes still on Rachel's blanket, imagining tucking the yellow one around Hannah the same way. Rachel's blanket clips are clear plastic. I am admiring them when Mrs. Nevins says, "Come in, Ruthie—close the door, dear."

I look up at Mrs. Nevins. "I—I'm going to walk," I answer.

"But there's plenty of room." Mrs. Nevins smiles. I let the door slip out of my hand and it closes. I start down the stairway. The elevator moans as it passes the third, then the second floor. I catch a glimpse of Mrs. Nevins, looking puzzled, through the lit circle of the window. I hold the door open for her in the lobby. I smile again. Her lips part and she tilts her head. She takes a breath as if she wants to say something. Then her mouth closes and she smiles.

I'm thinking how much nicer she is than Joannie. I take the steps two at a time to the outside door.

The Kogen brothers are closing up as I pass. Simon is pulling down the iron gate. Abe nods and looks at me.

When I arrive at the butcher shop Benny Pitt is in the meat refrigerator putting away meat, getting ready to close. "Just a minute, Dahling!" he calls. I count salamis to pass the time. Six big, three small like the ones my mother buys. Benny Pitt beams at me from the refrigerator. "I don't know what I would have done without you, Ruthie—Mrs. Berman telephoned to say thank you," he calls in puffs of steam. Then he steps out of the refrigerator and follows my eyes to the salamis. His red cheeks look like red apples.

Then Benny Pitt's arm begins to reach up, moving higher until it touches the biggest salami. I watch as he lifts it off its hook. "A good worker deserves a good—salary!" says Benny Pitt. "Some good salami!" He puts the salami on his wooden block and cuts a slice three inches thick, snaps a piece of brown paper from its roll. He wraps the salami, puts it in a bag and hands it to me. "Dahling, wait. Let me take the bag of feet a minute, I'll put some gizzards for your mamma's soup—what a soup that will be!" I watch Benny Pitt, who seems to be moving in slow motion, and I can't believe what has happened. Salami, salami, salami, salami, is all I can think. Garlicky, greasy, salty, salami! And my mouth starts watering and I pinch my lips together so that it doesn't water down my chin. I swallow and pinch my mouth shut, swallow and pinch my mouth shut.

"What is it, Dahling? Do you want to eat it now?" Benny Pitt asks, looking puzzled.

"Oh—no—uh—thank you..." and suddenly I realize

81

I've never addressed Benny Pitt by name. I can't call him Benny, like Mamma does. "Thank you—uh—uh—Mr. —uh—Benny—uh—Mr.—uh—Mr. Pitt!" I finally get the words out of my watery mouth, trying to pinch my lips tight at the same time.

"You are very welcome, Ruthie Pincus," says Benny Pitt, handing me the two bags.

Now I have to hurry.

"Ruthie!" Benny Pitt calls before I close the door. "Ask your Mamma if you can help me again next Thursday when Moshe visits his sister in the Bronx! The day before Shabbes—Moshe has to go—the busiest day of the week! Ask your Mamma, Ruthie. I'll pay you fifty cents." I look at him. His apple smile is waiting—he nods. "Yes?" he asks. "Tell your Mamma you are a good worker! Tell her the butcher says so!"

Me? Me? I want to say. A job for me? "Oh, thank you, uh—Mr. Pitt! I'll ask my mother!"

Oh please, Mamma, Mamma, please, please, please, I'm chanting to the rhythm of my footsteps, hurrying down Crown Street. "Mamma!" I shout up the steps.

"Where have you been it's almost dark?" My mother shouts down. "I have a soup without feet!"

"Mamma, Mrs. Berman needed a pot roast to make her supper! I ran an errand for Benny Pitt!" I call up the steps.

"At night when your family is waiting you ran an errand?" Mamma's eyebrows are high.

"Mamma, it isn't dark yet—he paid me with—salami!"

"Paid you with—salami?" echoes my mother.

"Salami? SALAMI?" Georgie calls from the kitchen table.

"And he sent you gizzards for the soup! Benny Pitt

says I'm a good worker. He said I should tell you, Mamma. He wants me to work for him next Thursday—could I? Mamma I'll earn fifty cents! If I work the next week and the next I'll have enough with my allowance for the carriage set, enough to pay you back! Maybe we can ask Mr. Bender to hold the carriage set for two extra weeks!"

If it's possible my mother's eyebrows seem to move up higher. Her brown eyes are blinking. Then she says, "Pay me back?" Then her eyes narrow. When she speaks again her voice is quiet. "We don't talk business at supper! Wash your hands and sit down. It's bad enough the soup has no feet. Now it has no gizzards and it's getting cold!"

"Salami—Mamma, Salami? What salami?" demands Georgie.

"Rebecca, won't you have some soup with your egg salad, Sweetheart?" Mamma asks my sister.

"Mamma, you know I don't eat chicken!" answers my sister.

"Darling, there's hardly any chicken in it," says my mother.

"Mamma!" Rebecca puts down her fork.

"Darling, it isn't healthy," says my mother.

"Miriam, eggs are good food," says my father. "Eat your supper, Rebecca."

My mother looks at my father and sighs. She puts the chicken feet and gizzards into the freezer. She unwraps the salami and brings it to the table on a plate. She puts it between my dish of fricassee and my bowl of soup. "This is special for Ruthie," says Mamma. "It's her—salary." My brother Georgie laughs. Then he looks confused. "That's not celery, Mamma, it's salami! I can see it! Salami!" Now his mouth is puckering and his eyes are filling with tears. My mother looks at me. She looks so tired. "Here, Georgie," I tell my brother. I cut him a piece and put it on

83

his plate. Leon's eyebrows are raised. I cut him a piece too. Rebecca looks disgusted.

"A job!" says my father, smiling. He's looking at me, sitting back in his chair.

"It sounds so grown up," says Leon, around a mouth full of salami.

"Leon," says my mother. "Don't talk with your mouth full!"

Rebecca turns her head away. "Grown up?" says Rebecca looking at me with her sour face. "Who plays with dolls at ten years old?"

"I'm still nine," I answer. My eyes sting and I'm thinking how much I want to take my father's suggestion and call Rebecca a peasant. I can feel the word rising in my throat next to the hot lump, peasant, peasant, when suddenly Mamma speaks instead.

"Rebecca," she announces quietly. "I played with my doll until I was—fourteen." My father turns to my mother. So does Rebecca.

Oh, did you, Mamma? I'm thinking. Did you really? In my stomach I feel a flood of warm. I look at my sister now. She's frowning, eating her egg salad and won't look at me. The word, peasant, has floated up to the ceiling. Peasants are farmers, I can hear Donna say. And farmers are good.

"Fourteen, Mamma?" I ask as we wash the dishes after supper. My mother smiles, her cheeks are pink. "What was her name?" I ask.

"Her name?" repeats my mother, looking surprised. Her head tilts and she laughs suddenly. "It was Bluma!"

"Bluma?" I repeat.

"It's Yiddish. It means flower. Bluma," she says again, then we're silent, me looking at Mamma, Mamma looking at the kitchen curtains.

"Bennie Pitt said Mrs. Berman had no one to send,

Mamma," I say after a moment.

Mamma sighs, turns to me and nods.

"Can—can we talk about business now?" I ask.

My mother begins putting away dishes, opening and closing cabinets. She puts a pot into the pot drawer, rattling it against the others. She takes the rag from the faucet and scrubs the sink and rinses it. Then she pours cleanser on the sponge and scrubs the sink again. She polishes the faucet with the dishtowel and finally looks up. "Well?" she asks.

"Can I? Can I deliver meat for Benny Pitt on Thursday?"

Mamma sighs. "You can," she says. Then she takes the broom from the closet. She sweeps the kitchen with hard, short strokes. And I'm not sure I've heard. "Can?" I repeat, thinking she meant to say "can't". But she nods.

I pull in my breath. "Mamma, what if he asks about the following Thursday?"

Now Mamma looks at me. "Is that what he said?" she asks.

"He said Moshe visits his sister on Thursdays. He said it's his busiest day—because of Shabbes."

Mamma nods. Then she turns to me and puts the broom down. "Do you want to say yes?" she asks.

I nod.

"Then you'll say yes," says my mother.

I want to dance. I want to twirl to the rhythm of the Tarantella, the yellow plastic record Pappa plays for Georgie on the record player. I'm nodding and I'm nodding and I'm nodding. "And can we ask Mr. Bender to hold the carriage set for two more weeks?"

"No!" says Mamma. "But I won't have enough—"

"Listen," says my mother. "I'll advance you the money. You'll iron your father's shirts. I'll pay seven cents a shirt. That will save us three cents and a trip to Schenectady

85

Avenue. You can start tomorrow, I'll show you how—if you want to—"

Then I'm thanking my mother and hugging her. She's squeezing me and we're laughing. Then Mamma lets me go and gives me a long, serious look. "Ruthie, I'm proud of you," she tells me. "Mrs. Berman is all by herself. You did something good." She picks up the broom again. She sweeps then stops and leans her forehead on the broomstick. She takes out her handkerchief and pinches her nose. Her eyes fill up. "Soon you'll be old enough to stay with Georgie," she tells me.

I go to Bender's the following Friday and buy the carriage set. On the way home I stop at Nat's Candy Store. I look into the glass nickel machine. A pink doll is right near the bottom. I put in my nickel and turn the handle. A plastic capsule falls with a thud. Inside is a green, rubber snake. When I get home I jiggle the snake near Hannah. "Isn't this unusual?" I ask Hannah.

"But wait until you see this!" I tell her. Then I unwrap the carriage set. I hold it to my face. It smells like Bender's, like new clothes and polished floors. I unfold the blanket. "Oh, Hannah, isn't it beautiful?" I take the blanket that was Leon's then Rebecca's then mine, then Georgie's, fold it and put it on my dresser.

"And won't these look pretty when you're in the carriage on the porch—or maybe in the porch room? It's sunny there." I hold up the sweater and hat and tortoise shell clips for her to see. For now I tuck them into my drawer. Of course we won't go walking, I'm thinking. Not at nine, almost ten. Joannie Nevins and Aylene Muntzer probably wouldn't understand. But how perfect Hannah will look in her carriage in the sunlight streaming through the porch room windows while she naps. I remember the way Mrs. Nevins tucked the blanket around Rachel. I tuck the yellow blanket around Hannah, just imagining sitting in the porch room sun next to the carriage, pasting dog pictures, and doing my homework.

A Bird House

Passing the telephone building at the corner of Troy Avenue, on the way to school, Aylene Muntzer catches up to me.

"How's your new collection?" says Aylene, smiling with one corner of her mouth. Her glittering, green snake eyes are waiting for me to answer. I'm wondering how Aylene knows I'm collecting rocks. I look at her. I want to tell her, Oh, I'm just looking for a fossil, using my father's shirt cardboards since I don't have five dollars to buy a set of rocks like you did, Aylene, but really, rock hunting in the alley is much more fun than handing five dollars to the woman behind the counter at the museum, you know? I want to say that. I think of the clear, yellow amber in Aylene's set, and the blue lapis lazuli and my chest aches with longing. None of your beeswax, Aylene, is what I want to say, but I just tilt my mouth to look like hers and keep walking.

"Your fat, how is it?" Aylene asks next. I stop walking. I look straight ahead. Did I hear her?

Then she says, "I heard it smelled bad."

I turn and look at her. She stops too. The side of her mouth is still smiling, slanting over the top of her books. "Who ever heard of collecting fat?" she asks, snorting out a laugh.

I don't move. My stomach starts gurgling. I feel like grabbing Aylene and shaking her. "How do you know?" I ask.

87

"Your sister told my brother that you have a fat collection from the butcher's. Everyone knows."

I can hardly see Aylene or the buildings or the sidewalk because weird shapes are moving through the air, sparkling. My heart is pounding. My lips are opening. A word flies past them. "Peasant!" It comes up from some place in my throat. It's the word my father tells me to call Rebecca when she calls me stupid or ugly, flat face and fat nose. "That's a Berman nose!" My mother tells Rebecca then. And my mother might then kiss it, my nose, even if it's running. "Please, Mamma," I say as she pulls the photo album from the breakfront drawer and shows me and Rebecca a picture of herself when she was my age, standing with Aunt Dorothy and Grandma Anna, whose hair is dark instead of white. "That's your great grandmother Yetta's nose," says Mamma then. And I look at the picture of Mamma and see that our noses are the same. So are our eyes and mouths. Then I feel as if I'm looking at myself. "The Bermans are strong, Ruthie. You can be proud of that nose!" says my mother, and tells my sister not to make fun of it, or her ancestors and, really, her own nose as well. But Rebecca's nose is taller at the bridge, and slimmer, like our grandfather's.

And that word Pappa tells me to call Rebecca when she calls me one of those names, that word "Peasant!" the word I've just called Aylene Muntzer is now hanging in the air, sounding in my ears.

Aylene is laughing, with both sides of her mouth. "What did you say?" says Aylene.

"I said, peasant. Peasant, that's what I said, Aylene, and that's what you are! A—farmer—a peasant!"

"Huh?" Aylene's mouth droops. "A farmer—?"

"Now get out of my way," I tell Aylene. Her eyebrows have vanished under the blond hair that hangs on her forehead as I push past her toward school.

Mrs. Roth tells us we'll spend our science time preparing for the Fair. She asks us to write a report: "My Science Fair Project," in forty five minutes. We're supposed to outline our goals.

I sit at my desk drawing in the margins of my loose leaf paper. Mrs. Roth will write a note about it to my mother. She'll write it at the top of my paper in red pen. "Please present your papers appropriately," it will read. Mamma will have to sign it, again. But I still don't know whether I'm going to do the rubber band ball, or get more fat at the butcher's and see if any birds come to the back yard to eat it.

My rock collection is, well, limited—mostly white quartz. White Quartz of New York State? I'm thinking. I don't know. If I go rock hunting a few more times maybe I'll find something interesting, like a fossil, or a geode. I draw circles, one inside the other, until the smallest circle is only a dot. I draw a big circle next to it and color it in. How will I get enough rocks by two weeks from this Wednesday? Is one little fossil too much to ask?

Donna has homework, so I spend the afternoon in the alley alone. The Solloway's dog, Captain, dozes. I think he's gotten bored with the sound of smashing rocks. Most of the rocks I find are white quartz. Then things take a turn for the better. I find another piece of pink and black granite, and this one has a gold streak in it, then some gray rocks with bits of mica schist. Then I find a lot of white quartz and decide to go home early.

Captain is still sleeping when I pass. He opens one eye and snorts at me. His legs start moving but his eye closes. Captain is dreaming. I stop. I try to imagine what a German Shepherd might dream about. Bones? A good steak? But I can't imagine the Solloways serving Captain a steak. And how can he find a bone if he's always chained? Captain's legs are moving as if he's running. Now something catches in my throat. I'm suddenly thinking—he's dreaming of breaking free! That's what I'd be dreaming if I were Captain. I'd be dreaming of finding someplace else to live, instead of with Mr. and Mrs. Solloway. Captain opens an eye and takes a snorty breath. Then his fast asleep again, his legs going.

"Poor guy," I say softly. Captain's eye opens again. It looks at me. His eye is focusing. He's waking up. He growls. I'd be doing the same thing, I'm thinking, if I had to live in the Solloway's yard. I'm thinking this as I'm backing away. Captain's gotten to his feet. He starts barking. I hear Mrs. Solloway's window open. Hear her call, "Ruthie Pincus!" as I hurry down the alley toward home.

In the encyclopedia there's a picture of a rock that looks a lot like the pink and black granite. "Hornblende, feldspar, quartz and mica," reads the caption. By Tuesday I have eleven different kinds of rocks, counting a piece of coal from the basement. Twelve, counting the brick that has a shell. If I put six on a shirt cardboard that will almost make two trays. Georgie wanders into my room looking for one of his marbles.

"What would I be doing with your marble, Georgie?" I ask, not that patiently. I can see his face twitch. "Georgie," I say to distract him. "Look at my rock collection."

My brother looks blank. "What are they?" he asks. "Rocks, Georgie, maybe for my science fair project," I explain, but my voice sounds high. "Rocks?" repeats my brother. "Yes, rocks, Georgie, you know, stones. I found them in the alley." Georgie looks at me. I can see he's thinking. "What's a science project?" he asks next. I look at my brother. He's waiting for an explanation. "It's something for school," I tell him patiently. "To display in the gym." My brother is silent. "To play in the gym?" he asks. "No, Georgie," I answer. "To display in the gym. It's a display." "What's a display?" he asks next. My stomach is getting tight. "A—dis—Georgie, they'll sit on a table in the gym with the other science projects so that people can look at them."

"But who would want to look at a bunch of broken rocks?" asks Georgie. He shrugs, turning his palms upward. I can see he's sincere. "Georgie—" I say, a little irritably. His lower lip trembles. My brother Georgie is confused. "But who would, Rooty?" he asks. "Georgie, I don't know who would!" I admit, just a little too loudly. A sob escapes from Georgie's throat. Then I hear Mamma in the hall outside my room.

"Georgie, it's time for your nap," says our mother. "Come," she says, holding out her hand. "I'll read you a story." Georgie buries his head in Mamma's stomach and falls apart. When Georgie needs a nap he's sensitive. "Georgie, I'm sorry," I try to tell him. My mother picks him up. He wails down the hall to his room, and I hear Mamma close his door.

My mind starts racing. Maybe I'll just glue four rocks to each piece of cardboard. That would at least make three trays. I could use doubles, pieces that have more feldspar and some that have more hornblende. I could do a few trays of white quartz. I could write about the way the white quartz breaks up differently each time I find a piece and hit it with the hammer, depending on how you aim and how hard you smash them. I could tell about how most rocks in Brooklyn seem to be white quartz. I could explain how exciting it is to spot a rock that looks just like the geodes at the museum, then smashing it, and seeing—well—more white quartz! I sit down on my bed and lean against the wall.

Georgie is right. Who's going to want to look at a bunch of broken rocks? The Science Fair is getting nearer and I don't know what I'm going to do. Now I feel like crying. The rubber band ball? The fat? Why doesn't Mrs. Roth ever give us enough time?

Then Rebecca is at my door. "Here," she's saying. She's holding out a pendant she made in camp, a turquoise stone wrapped in copper wire. "You can use the stone for your rock collection."

I just look at her. "But—but you made it," I say.

"I never wear it," she answers.

"Ruthie-I'm-sorry-about-about your fat collection." My sister, Rebecca, is looking right into my eyes.

"You told Aylene's brother," I say, frowning.

Rebecca flushes and looks away. I hear her take a breath. Then she looks at me again. "I shouldn't have," she says.

It must be Sam, Rebecca's boyfriend, I'm thinking, because the only time my sister apologizes is when Pappa tells her she has to.

Rebecca smiles. And I smile too.

The turquoise stone is Chrysocolla. I find a picture of it in the encyclopedia.

92

Thursday, shopping for my mother at Benny Pitt's, watching him trim fat from the stew meat, I am worrying. I can't think of anything but finding a geode or a fossil. There were fossils at the museum that came from New York State. Brooklyn is in New York State, I'm thinking. If only I could find a trilobite, or even a fossil of a shell, not in a brick, but in a rock, like Aylene Muntzer's.

I stand at Benny Pitt's wooden block imagining wrapping a blanket around an ordinary gray stone, smashing, opening the blanket, seeing the two halves fall open and a petrified trilobite lodged in one half and imprinted in the other. It happens in slow motion and I feel like giggling. "Two!" I whisper, then realize I've spoken. Benny Pitt is looking at me, holding out a handful of trimmed fat. "More than two, Dahling, there's at least ten good pieces here. The sweetest suet in the world! You'll have a back yard full of birds. They'll come from New Jersey, you'll see!"

"But the last fat, it—" The butcher has already wrapped it up and put it into the bag with the stew meat.

"You have maybe a bird house?" he asks.

"A bird house?" I repeat. If I had a bird house it would be more like a real science project. They'd have a house of their own! I could make a list of bird names. I could draw bird pictures and staple them together. "I could draw a picture of the bird house for the cover!" And I realize that I've said this out loud too.

"Sure!" agrees the butcher, handing me the bag of meat and fat. "They don't all fly south. And the ones that stay the winter, are they *hungry*, Dahling!"

Something Simple

"What's that?" my mother asks, looking at the wax paper bag in my hand.

I look down at the bag. "This?" I answer. I look up at my mother. Mamma's eyes grow. They look dark, her pupils large. She's leaning toward the bag. "Yes, this," she says, reaching for it. But I pull it back.

"Ruthie, what is it, where did you get it?"

But Mamma knows. She's scowling. There's a crease between her eyebrows.

"Mamma, Benny Pitt gave it to me. It's for—the birds—it's fresh, Mamma. I'm going to put it in the back yard for them."

My sister, Rebecca, is grating potatoes into a bowl for Mamma's potato pudding, her kugal. Mamma's and Grandma Anna's, passed from my Great Grandmother Yetta and people I don't know the names of, but who are our family. People long ago in Lithuania who grew potatoes, who were farmers. Who were peasants. That's what my grandmother has told me.

But Rebecca has stopped grating and is turned toward my mother and me. She's holding a potato in mid air, strings of white pulp dangling from it. Rebecca has Pappa's hazel eyes. They're looking at us, wide, light circles.

"It's—just—fat," I say to my mother, but I'm looking at Rebecca.

Rebecca looks odd. She's still holding that potato and now her eyes are gazing. "Just fat," I see her lips say, rather than hear her, because I think she may be saying this to herself. Then she swallows. She's remembering, I'm pretty sure. Remembering the smell of old socks and moldy sneakers and the way that smell filled the house when I forgot to take out the last bag of fat for the birds the butcher sent me home with, and it turned rancid. I'm pretty sure that's what she's thinking because her face is starting to look a little green. Rebecca puts the potato down. She puts her hand to her mouth and groans. "I—Mamma, I think I'm—going to be sick—"

"Not while you're making my supper!" declares my mother, hurrying over to Rebecca, pulling her away from the bowl of grated potatoes. "Ruthie, put that—that—fat into the refrigerator!" she says glaring at me.

I jam the paper bag behind the vegetable bin, the same place where my mother hides salami. I push the bin as far back as it will go hoping Mamma and Rebecca will just forget about it. I walk down the hall to my room. I don't have enough rocks, I'm thinking, but a bird house, a bird house, a bird house. How hard could it be to make one?

Pappa's door is closed. I can hear the typewriter. I knock. The typewriter keys are clicking. I knock again. I open the door, slowly, and stand in the doorway. My father is frowning down at the typewriter, concentrating, popping the keys, typing with two fingers. The typewriter keys sound like the subway train wheels speeding along their tracks, they strike the paper so fast. One clackity sound. My father types faster with two fingers than Leon types with all his ten.

Hello, Pappa, I want to say, how is your science article coming along? I'm sorry to disturb your work but I was thinking, isn't Science wonderful? Practically anything you can think of is Science, Pappa, don't you agree? That's all, Pappa. I just knew you must feel the same way and wanted to tell you! I actually want to say all this, knowing I should not be opening my father's door while he's working. Knowing the door is closed because he does not want to be disturbed.

Then I blurt out, "Pappa, I need to build a birdhouse. Benny Pitt suggested I do. He said it could hold suet and they'd come—think of it! From New Jersey, Pappa, all that way! The birds, Pappa—it's for the birds!"

"Hmmmmmm?" says my father, his eyes flickering up at me then back to the paper in the typewriter with no break in the smooth clacking roll, looking like a pianist, graceful like Aunt Rose playing Beethoven or Mozart or Franz Liszt or Chopin. But tomorrow he'll look like the stunt piano players on television, the ones dressed in tuxedos and gowns, hunched over like strange, grinning runners, playing for speed not beauty. But Pappa will be dressed as he is now, in his worn brown corduroy pants and the moccasins he shuffles around the house in. And he won't be grinning. His article is due in the morning.

"A birdhouse, Pappa! A bird house!" I'm saying, my hand on the door knob. "I need one for my science project!" My stomach is jumping and I know I should close the door again and wait until tomorrow, when the door won't be closed, to tell this to my father. I feel out of control, like Georgie must feel when he needs a nap. "The Science Fair is next Wednesday, Pappa!" The words are flying out of me. They're rushing out of my mouth even though I know that this room is my father's office when other fathers are gone all day and their children can't ask them for help if they need to. I'm talking about building a bird house knowing that soon my father will be playing those keys for speed not beauty! "Wednesday?" he says as if he's talking in his sleep. "Sugarplum," he murmurs, his pointers flying like humming birds, "I'll be up half the night working as it is or we'd build one—what—happened—to the—rocks?" he asks, glancing hastily up, without missing a clack, smacking the carriage handle each time the bell rings to start a new line, his eyes slipping away from me again, back to the paper curling up out of the typewriter.

"I might not have enough rocks—Pappa, I'll build it, not really build it, just—I'll sort of—put it together. Just something simple they—the birds—may like!" I tell him. "I just need something that they—would like to—to—stop at, and, maybe, rest awhile, to take a little break from—uh, flying—to have a snack, say—something to eat that's sweet. New Jersey is far!"

"New Jersey?" asks my father, hitting the carriage return again. "Who?" he says, his eyes flicking to mine then down again.

"The birds," I answer. Then I just stand there.

Pappa's typing slows. He raises his head. He looks a little confused. He looks from the paper to me, me to the paper. Me. Paper. Me. Then he stops typing. He takes off his glasses. Then he sits there really looking at me, blinking, and his eyes begin to take on life.

"Just something I can put the fat on—," I say, letting go of the doorknob and crossing to his desk. "Then I can draw pictures of the birds that come to eat it, and label them for my Birds of New York State project—and maybe New Jersey. Benny Pitt said birds love fat. He said it's sweet—like candy—but for birds. Like bird chocolate."

My father is curling his fingers, running them through his hair like a comb, moving them over the top of his head so the hairs separate, some parts going one way, some the other. "You'll draw pictures of birds?" he asks. Then he smiles. He's thinking of my drawings. Then his forehead wrinkles up. "Honey doll, my deadline..." he says.

"Pappa, I know how to hammer! I just need some nails and wood!"

Now my father's eyes are beginning to light up because my father loves to make things, the way I do.

97

"Some nails and wood," he says. He nods. Then he looks out the window in the direction of the back yard. He's begun to think about it. He picks up a pencil and scribbles on a piece of paper. "Bird house." "A piece of plywood and a post would make—a platform," he says. "It needs to be high so they can see it, the birds."

I'm nodding like crazy. My father is scribbling a picture of a platform and a post.

"You have to join them together," he's saying. I know he wishes he could help me. He leans back in his chair and smiles again.

"Pappa, I'll figure it out!" I cry. That brings my mother hurrying down the hall. "Shhh!" she's scolding. "If Georgie wakes up now we'll have no peace! Ruthie! Your father is working!"

"Thank you!" I'm whispering to my father.

"Look in the garage—" Pappa says softly. "There are some fence posts, a few boards—" he's scratching his head. "Look in the nail jar, on the shelf, Ruthie." Then he turns to my mother. "It will be very pleasant, Miriam. We'll see birds through the window. It will be good for the children. Ruthie's creative!" All this he says softly, not to wake my brother, Georgie.

My mother and I look at each other as I slip past her out the door. Mamma just looks tired.

Wings

I rummage in the garage, find the nails and fence posts and some boards. Perfect, I think, choosing a board and a post. I stand the post and hold the board. I hammer in a nail. It goes in perfectly.

"There!" I say with satisfaction. But the nail is too short. It doesn't hold. "Okay, a longer nail," I'm saying out loud. I find one in the jar. It bends in half when I hit it with the hammer. I find another. This one bends too. It's a struggle to get these out, using the prongs at the back of the hammer. But I do it.

"Hmm," I'm murmuring. My neck is getting sweaty. I unbutton my jacket. I find another long nail and concentrate. I hit it carefully. "This is harder than I thought it would be," I'm saying, but the nail is sinking deeper into the wood, then it's in. It's holding. I hammer in a second nail, and a third. The board and post are joined!

I step back to look at it. It doesn't look exactly like a house, I'm thinking, more like a lean-to. "A bird lean-to," I say quietly, than I'm nodding, fairly sure the birds will like it. There's plenty of room for them to land, I'm thinking, plenty of space to line up the suet. I can imagine those beautiful white squares, calling to them like the candy store counter, saying swee-eee—eeet! Swee-eee-eet! The way Benny Pitt does. "Yum," I say, the way I used to when I fed Georgie, so he'd open his mouth. "Mmmmm, yummy," I'm whispering, nodding at the thing I've nailed together, beginning to admire it, thinking how really interesting it looks. It will be good to draw for my science project, I'm thinking. It just wiggles a bit. So I try adding some thicker nails, which are harder to hammer in, but it doesn't stop it from being wiggly. Next I try hammering in a couple of nails diagonally.

I spend the next half hour hammering nails into zigzags and U shapes until I finally give up. "I'll have to wait for Pappa," I tell myself very firmly. Then I imagine knocking softly at his door, telling him there is just one more teeny-weeny thing my bird house needs so that the birds can use it safely and not fall off because it wobbles and so that the Lamont's cat and the strays that wander the alley won't mistake the birds and falling suet for their supper. Ruthela, doll, I can imagine him saying, we'll do it tomorrow. "His article," I say to the garage. And I know how my mother's face would look if I knocked on my father's door again.

"My father is at work," I tell myself quietly, as if I'm giving my doll, Hannah, a good talking to. Even if he's really sitting in his room, at his desk, in his chair, right here at our own house on Crown Street. Learn patience, Ruthie, I can imagine him saying, the way he does when I'm looking for something in my drawers and can't find it, and throw a few things onto the floor. Or when I'm pulling things from my closet, talking sternly, maybe even raising my voice a little at a hanger as if it was an actual person. "His article his article, his article," I'm saying, trying to help myself be patient. Don't disturb your father when he's writing, I can hear my mother tell me. It's our livelihood! Maybe I could just walk down the hall to his room just to show him my bird house, maybe wobble it a bit, maybe not even ask him anything about it. Unless he asks me *why* it wobbles. But I'm bound to meet Mamma in the kitchen.

It's already getting dark, I think. Then there's sleeping. Then it will be morning, then school, then home and by then Pappa will be done with his article.

The next day Pappa says the wobbling might be just what the birds would enjoy, the way they enjoy the swaying branches of trees. But he adds shims, and bolts on metal diagonals, to steady the platform. "In case the suet brings a crowd," he tells me.

The cold has made the ground hard. Pappa is remarking as he tries to dig, that if we'd waited until the spring it wouldn't take us an hour and a half to open up a simple hole in the dirt of the ground of our back yard for the fence post. I explain to my father that the Science Fair is next Wednesday and spring would be too late. Also, I remind him, that in spring the birds can find their own food so why would they want to stop by my bird house to eat?

My father tells me that of course he understands all of that, and that it's hard to think logically when the wind is blowing, say, thirty-five or maybe forty miles an hour and it's twenty-three degrees and looks like it might snow. Pappa and I take turns digging. When it's my turn I jump on the shovel to add my weight. Between the two of us, slowly, very slowly, very very slowly, we chip away the dirt with the shovel. So slowly that I am shivering and my father's lips are beginning to look a little blue, we're carving out a hole deep enough to hold a post. Finally my father stands the post into the hole.

"We need stones to brace this," he says, looking around. But there are no stones in the back yard, just the iris bed and the Rose of Sharon bush and the dried up grass.

"The alley, Pappa," I say. My father nods, breathing steam. "I'll hurry," I tell him. I take the shovel into the alley and pry up a piece of broken asphalt. I hear Captain's chain jingle. He comes out of his dog house and sees me. I smile at him. "Hello, boy," I call softly. Captain gives one short bark and sits down, panting steam. Maybe he can see I'm trying to be nice to him. I kick the broken asphalt and find two big stones. I load them onto the shovel then haul them back to my father whose glasses are starting to mist up. "Better get one more," he says.

Captain's voice is higher as I enter the alley again. He's straining against his collar, at the end of his chain. I look over at him. Suddenly he sits down. "Good dog, Captain," I say quietly. Low in his throat he growls.

I find a smooth gray stone that I think looks like granite. Probably more white quartz, I'm thinking as Mrs. Solloway raises her window and glares at me. I pick the stone up and tuck the shovel under my arm as I pass Captain. He's watching me. I smile at him, hoping Mrs. Solloway can see me. Captain just sits there looking at me. But he isn't growling, which I consider progress.

"Ruthie!" my father calls from the back yard, and now he's walking in my direction. "Is that dog tied up?" Then he sees it's Mrs. Solloway's dog and he sees Mrs. Solloway. "Hello, Captain," he says quietly. Then he nods to Mrs. Solloway. "It's only us, David Pincus and my daughter Ruthie. How are you, Mrs. Solloway?" Steam is coming out of Pappa's mouth as he says this.

"What are you doing, Mr. Pincus?" asks Mrs. Solloway.

"We're putting up a bird house," Pappa calls.

"A birdhouse?" repeats Mrs. Solloway. "Putting up a birdhouse in the middle of winter?"

Pappa nods and smiles. Now Captain starts barking.

"Quiet!" hollers Mrs. Solloway. She frowns and closes the window. But she doesn't slam it. I see her lips moving. Her lips look like they're repeating Pappa's words. They move like they might be saying birdhouse.

"Poor dog," Pappa says quietly.

Pappa and I head to the back yard, walking quickly against the wind. I drop the stone I've carried from the alley into the hole. It hits hard against the other stones and falls open in two perfect halves. In the late afternoon light I can see the outline of something on its surfaces. I pick up the pieces. "Pappa!" I cry. And the thing running through my head is that this stone isn't white quartz!

My father looks down at the stone in my hands. Then he looks up and our eyes catch and it feels as if we're holding onto each other through our eyes. Then I look back at the pieces of stone. Look look look look I want to say, how does an insect get into a rock in the middle of winter, Pappa, and what happened to the rest of it? This is what I want to say but all I can do is look from the two halves of stone in my hands and back at my father. Who drew this perfect thing? I want to say too, as my father bends over the thing in my hands and lifts his glasses to his forehead to look more closely. I don't really know where I am, if I'm outside in the back yard or in the museum or if I'm dreaming. There are just these duplicate impressions of an insect wing, and my two blue-gloved hands holding them, and my father.

"My God, Ruthie!" says Pappa. I think it's limestone—it looks like a dragon fly wing." Limestone, limestone, I'm saying inside, that will make thirteen different kinds of rocks, thirteen! Then I'm saying dragon fly, and the word is looping and buzzing in my head. And my father is just looking at these halves of stone, touching the delicate lines of the veins in their wings, turning them over as they rest in my hand. And he finally says it, "A fossil," and his voice is soft and breathless in a way I heard it once when we watched a star shoot clear across the sky over the back yard, just as we pulled into the garage after visiting my cousins in the Bronx. And it feels as if there's nothing but the beautiful, delicate lines of the wings sitting in the palms of my blue gloves and that sound in Pappa's voice.

"Ruthie! Right here in the back yard, a fossil! We're probably looking at two million years—" His face is shining, as if he's looking into the sun, as if someone is holding up a flashlight. His eyes are wide and his forehead seems big, like the sky. And when he lifts his head to look at me his eyes are catching the bright yellow of the winter afternoon. And he kisses me softly on the forehead. Then we say "a fossil!" We say it together and we laugh. "Pappa, two!" I say. "Two," my father repeats. "Imagine," he's saying, tracing the outlines with the tips of his fingers. "It could even be a locust," he murmurs.

"Pappa, my science project! I have a fossil—two fossils!"

"If the birds find this feeder you'll have two science projects!"

"Two! Two!" I'm saying.

"Look at this thing, Ruthie!" holding the wing images to the light. Two, two, two, just keeps singing inside. Two fossils and two science projects. Two two two two!

Friday in school I just keep thinking about the insect wing, going over the moment when the stone fell open. Two million years old, I'm thinking. Two fossils, two science projects. Two million years! Then I'm imagining the birds of New York State from my bird book, and maybe some from New Jersey, two states, two two two, flocking to my bird house in the back yard. Two, two... When Mrs. Roth calls on me I look up, and feel my cheeks go hot. "Two?" I murmur. Mrs. Roth's eyes are bright, looking at me. "Right," says Mrs. Roth. "Good, Ruthie!"

The thing is, I don't know what question I've just answered. In my eyes are images of insect wings in stone, and birds from New York and New Jersey nibbling at the pile of Benny Pitt's sweet suet.

Waiting

"Mamma!" I shout up the steps when I come home from school. "Did they come?"

"They? Who are we expecting?" demands my mother in a whisper. She's holding her finger to her lips. My little brother, Georgie, is napping.

"The birds—did they come for the suet?" I whisper back.

"As if I have time to look for birds!" whispers my mother, frowning. She pours me a glass of milk and stirs in chocolate syrup.

I sit in front of the window of my room, watching the plywood platform sitting on its fence post, the bird platform I've made, which Pappa and I have put up in the back yard. I'm sipping chocolate milk, waiting to write the names of birds on the lined, loose-leaf paper I've stapled together with colored paper covers to make my bird book. A sparrow lands on the garage roof and pecks at the shingles. He hops around, pecking. The wind brushes the feathers on his head and they stand up. He pecks again. "Shingles?" I say softly. "You think those are good? Wait until you taste the suet!" The sparrow has got something in its mouth. It looks like a wad of pollywogs, the seed pods that come spinning down in spring from the Maple tree, the things that I peel open, that have sticky stuff inside. I stick them onto my nose, the way everyone else who lives on Crown Street does, except, of course, the adults. For a minute I imagine Mr. Pukatch, Donna's father, with a pollywog on his nose, and maybe Mrs. Solloway. I smile, trying to think who else to picture until I realize the sparrow seems really to be enjoying these things. It tosses its little head and is definitely swallowing something.

Hmm, I'm thinking, maybe it's like eating salad. But what kind of salad is a clump of rotten pollywogs? Maybe they're more like spinach. Then I realize what I'm looking at. There *are* bugs in winter! And they're hidden in rotting pollywogs, like celery is hidden in tuna fish, or raisins in some people's coleslaw! Things I'd rather not find there. But clearly this sparrow is enjoying finding these bugs, if they are bugs. Hmm, that's interesting, I'm thinking. I could draw a picture of the sparrow eating the pollywogs. Sparrows, Pollywogs and The Hidden Bugs of Winter, isn't all that bad a science project if no other birds turn out for the suet.

I'm wondering how the sparrow knows the bugs are there. Maybe they make sounds that are too tiny except for birds to hear. That's interesting too. I don't see them, I don't hear them, but the sparrow, it knows that they're there! How? Maybe the sparrow can see them with its tiny bird eyes. I could write about that, exploring other possibilities. I don't know—I'm thinking, it's only that one sparrow. Then another one lands on the roof and starts poking at the pollywogs too.

I tap on the window to get their attention, to try to catch their eyes. The first one tilts its head, looking sideways, so all I can see is one black eye, looking up, looking down, looking around as if he hears me and is trying to see where the tapping is coming from. "You can see tiny bugs, can't you see me?" I say quietly. Can the birds hear my voice through the glass? I ask myself. "They can hear bugs, can't they?" I answer.

The first sparrow pecks at the shingles again. The other sparrow has hopped up to the peak of the roof and is checking out the shingles there. Maybe if I concentrate and think about the suet they'll get the idea. I decide to practice my mental telepathy with the sparrows the way my sister, Rebecca, says she practices hers on me.

Dessert, dessert, dessert, I start saying in my head. Suet, suet. I concentrate as hard as I can. The sparrows peck and tug at the pollywogs. Maybe if I talk to them directly, I think. I decide to open the window. I put my hands under the top sash and push as gently as I can, so the window won't lurch open and startle the sparrows, but it sticks. I push harder and it comes up suddenly. The weights that hold it knock and the window squeals. The first sparrow peeps and looks around, but doesn't fly away. The other one starts hopping along the roof peak, tilting its head like crazy. "There!" I call, trying to sound as friendly as I can. "Over there!" and now I'm scratching on the window screen. The sparrows fly away.

I want to eat supper at the window but Mamma says no. "It's dark," Rebecca tells me at the table. "Birds don't eat in the dark." Really? I think. What if they're hungry? I smile politely at my sister to keep from frowning. Bats eat in the dark, I'm thinking, why not birds? But I don't say it.

After supper I sit in front of the window in my room with the light off so that I can watch the feeder. Georgie wanders in and stands quietly next to me looking out too.

We both watch the dark silently. I feel my brother turn and look at me, then back out the window. At me, out the window. Then he sighs deeply. "Why are you just sitting here, Rooty?" he asks. "Georgie," I answer, groping for the 'B' encyclopedia lying on the floor next to me. I open it and turn a few pages. "Look at these pictures," I tell him. "I can't see anything!" says my brother. "Can't you see this one?" I ask, holding the book to the window where it catches the street lamp from the alley. "It's a grackle. See it?" "It's too dark!" says Georgie, sounding a little testy. "Look, Georgie, look at this robin." I point and hold the book close to my brother, keeping it tilted to catch the light. "What's this one?" asks Georgie. "Which?" I ask, looking at the encyclopedia then out the window. "THIS!" says my brother, startling me. "Georgie, if you shout they'll never come!" "Who?" Georgie asks. "The birds!" I follow his pointing finger. "That's an owl," I tell him. "Can we see one of those?" asks my brother. I look at him. "I don't think there are any owls in Brooklyn," I tell my brother. "But maybe there are," says Georgie. "Well, maybe," I say. "But I don't know if they eat suet." I'd never thought of owls. If there are none in Brooklyn there may be some in New Jersey. Then I'm considering how really amazing it would be if one showed up at the bird feeder. Wait, I'm thinking. Owls eat other birds! "That would be a catastrophe!" I say out loud. Georgie's eyes get round, and he looks out the window again. "Maybe we'll see one!" he declares, and he's whispering. "I'm sure there are no owls around here, Georgie," I say, hoping it's true. Georgie frowns. We both look out the window. "What's suet?" Georgie asks next.

"It's—fat," I tell him. "Fat?" he repeats, and I'm too tired to answer. I watch the silhouette of the feeder in the halo of the lamplight.

"Rooty," says Georgie after a moment. "Why are you just sitting here? Whyyyyy?" "Georgie, we're waiting," I tell him. "What forrrr?" asks my brother. I look at him. I know that if there's one thing Georgie doesn't understand it's waiting.

"Listen, Georgie," I tell him, lifting him and sitting him on my lap. "Look at this bird," I say, pointing to a picture of a purple finch. "But I can't see," says my brother. I hold the book back up to the window. My brother puts his face close to the book. "But it's not

108

purple!" he declares. Then he frowns. "Is there a picture of a frog?" he asks next. "Georgie, this is the B encyclopedia. A frog would be in the F!" Georgie's face collapses. This is getting to be too much of an effort, for both of us, I'm thinking.

But I don't give up. First I talk about the purple finch and how empty his tummy must feel, like Georgie when he shouts how hungry he is. I'm asking my brother to imagine that. Then I make up stories about the other birds in the pictures, and the way they are searching for food. How some very helpful people try to leave food for them, as I've left the suet that we're watching, white and chunky, on my bird platform beyond the window where we are sitting right now.

I'm holding the book up to the light of the street lamp, turning the pages. Then I come to the end of the article where all the species in the bird section of the encyclopedia are pictured in one, spectacular, two-page sky. I'm about to tell Georgie that these birds have obviously all finally eaten and are flying with joy when my brother starts shouting. "Wow! Wow! It's a jamboree!" He's shouting about the two pages in the encyclopedia. Georgie has a book called "The Frog Jamboree," about tree frogs and bull frogs and all the other frogs in the forest that come out at night to sing, some of them high-pitched, sweet, baby sounds, others croaking their songs, sounding as if they're plucking rubber bands into a microphone. Their pictures are all over the pages of Georgie's book. "It's a jamboree! A JAMBOREEE!" he just keeps saying. "Look, Georgie," I tell my brother, pointing to the purple finch, trying to keep him calm. "Think of how hungry he must feel if he can't find food!" Georgie looks at the picture. He's quiet.

Then, suddenly he slips off my lap. "Mamma!" he

109

calls. " I'm hungry! Mamma!" Georgie's heading for the hall. "Mamma, I'm feeling hungry!"

Saturday, while my parents visit my Aunt Rose, I work on my rock collection in front of the window. I look through the 'R' encyclopedia for pictures of insect fossils, trying to identify my fossil wing. All I find are trilobites and snails. I write "Rare Fossil" on a label I've made from Pappa's yellow school paper and put the two halves of the stone with the insect wing in a cardboard box that's lined with absorbent cotton. I rule lines on Pappa's shirt cardboards and glue down some other stones. I make a liverwurst sandwich and eat it in front of the window. The platform stands above the iris bed offering Benny Pitt's suet to the air.

Jamboree

My little brother, Georgie, has a book called "Frog Jamboree," about all the kinds of frogs in the world. Every species known to Science is pictured in Georgie's book. Georgie loves this book, and someone, myself, my mother, my father, my sister, my older brother, has to read it to Georgie before he will agree to go to sleep. It has been this way for months, ever since Aunt Loolie gave it to him for his third birthday.

Lately Georgie wants to hear it more than once. Sometimes Mamma and Pappa have to take turns reading it. My parents, particularly my father, want to encourage Georgie to love books and to read. Georgie certainly loves "Frog Jamboree," and if no one can read it to him Georgie turns the pages and pretends that he is reading it himself.

He's heard it so many times he practically knows it by heart. But sometimes Georgie improvises. For instance he may begin to read things about frogs that get bigger and bigger, not stopping in the usual way frogs do but getting, for instance, as big as a building or even filling the sky. Then of course it's necessary for the frogs to compete for space. Georgie usually names one the frog king and takes it from there.

When he tells these things to my parents they try to dissuade Georgie about his fondness for such conflicts. Particularly Pappa, who often says it's important to love peace.

On the last page of "Frog Jamboree" all the frogs in the world come out of all the trees and all the ponds and all the lakes and all the mud holes, and dance in front of the moon. That's their jamboree. It's like a terrific frog party. So when Georgie sees a swarm of flies, or a crowd of ants he calls it a jamboree. A fly or ant jamboree.

When we hit a traffic jam on our way to the Bronx, Georgie calls it a car jamboree. Right now it's just Georgie's thing. The way "shook-like-a-bowl-full-of-jelly" from "The Night Before Christmas" was his thing last year, so that when someone was laughing—say company, or someone in a store—Georgie would begin to shout, "shook-like-a-bowl-full-of jelly!" the way Saint Nicholas' stomach does in the poem. Though we all tried to discourage him, Georgie just liked the way the words sounded together, the way he now likes the sound of the word "jamboree."

Jamboree! Jamboree! Jamboreeeee! yelled Georgie at the football team's victory parade at the high school, when our brother Leon's team won the season. Jamboree! Georgie just kept shouting to Leon as he passed our blanket on the grass where we sat watching the parade.

Then, when Leon just kept moving with the parade, Georgie began to cry, shrieking the word jamboree until Leon had to come back and pick Georgie up and march in the parade holding him, while Georgie just kept calling, JAMBOREEE!

"Hey! Heyyy! HEYYY!" Georgie is yelling now, waking up from his nap. Hay is for horses, Georgie, I'm thinking. Why does this family have to be so emotional?

"Heyy!" Georgie yells again. "Heyy, heyy, heyy, heyyy!" Then I glance out my window. "My gosh, they're here!" I whisper. "They're here! Mamma!" and now I'm yelling up the hall toward the kitchen. "They came! They came! The back yard is mobbed with them! Oh, my gosh, Mamma, Pappa, look at them!" I'm calling into the hall.

"What's the matter with you?" says my mother, hurrying toward my room. "Have you lost your mind? You'll wake your brother!"

"A jamboree!" Georgie is calling. "A Bird Jamboreee! Mamma!"

"Mamma, look!" I'm saying, jumping up and down.

"MAM-MA! JAMBOREEEE!" Georgie is now screaming at the top of his lungs.

"Georgie, calm down!" calls my mother.

"JAMBOREEEE!" he's shrieking. Then he's laughing. Then he's crying, crazed as he usually is when he first wakes up.

Oh, my gosh, Georgie, no! I'm thinking now. No! No! No! They've finally come and my brother is going to scare them away! "Welcome to the Crown Street Lunatic Asylum," I say to the window glass in the direction of the bird feeder. Then my mouth just falls open because there are so many birds, and more just keep coming. "Gosh! It is a jamboree!" I'm murmuring.

My mother has reached Georgie.

112

The study door opens. "What is it?" my father is asking.

"BII-IIRDS!" Georgie's sobbing.

"Pappa, the birds found the feeder! They're eating the suet. Benny Pitt was right, Pappa, they love it!" I'm calling.

"That's good, Ruthie," says my father. "I have two hours to finish this article." He closes his door.

"Darn!" says my brother, Leon, from the bathroom. He opens the bathroom door. "What's going on?" There's shaving cream on his face, except for a diagonal path from his cheek to his chin. A piece of toilet paper is glued to the corner of his mouth, with blood.

My father's study door opens again. Pappa's carrying his typewriter. He's got a pencil in his mouth, a pile of typing paper is tucked under his arm. He heads toward the basement door. He's grumbling, mostly in Yiddish, but I hear the word "jamboree."

"Sha, Georgie, sha," my mother is saying to my brother. "Sha, darling. See the birds? Aren't they nice?" she's asking, sounding a little doubtful. "They're nice," my brother whimpers.

"They're here, they're here, they're here," I'm saying, pulling out crayons, trying to draw birds and turn the pages of the B encyclopedia at the same time. "He was right, he was right, Benny Pitt was right!" I'm saying. "Look at them all!" And I really can't believe it. Then Leon, holding his face and Mamma holding Georgie are standing next to me, looking out the window at the birds. The birds are squawking, peeping, tweeting, diving for Benny Pitt's suet.

"There must be two hundred birds!" calls my father from below us. He clatters up the basement steps, bursts through the basement door into the kitchen and rushes down the hall to my room. "Where's the Polaroid?" he's saying.

"Leon, didn't you borrow it to photograph your football team?" says Mamma.

"Leon!" shouts Pappa. "Where's the camera? Maybe three hundred!" he says, looking out the window in my room. "I'm glad I braced that thing!"

"My God," exclaims my mother. "Are all the windows closed?"

Leon has rushed across the hall to his room. I hear him rummaging through his closet. His cleats land in the hallway.

"LEON!" shouts my father. "That camera cost a fortune!"

Leon's football helmet rolls out of his room and stops next to his cleats. "It's here somewhere—oh for—ahhhhh!" cries my brother in a muffled voice. When he appears again there are big patches of skin showing through clumps of shaving cream. The bloody tissue is still stuck to the corner of his mouth. He's covering his eye with one hand, with the other he hands the Polaroid camera to my father. "This stuff stings!" says Leon.

"Don't rub it," exclaims my mother, "it will make it worse!"

"Leon, wash your eye in the sink—" says Pappa. Leon hurries across the hall to the bathroom and the cold water tap squeals.

"A bird jamboree!" Georgie is calling, his voice shrill. "JAMBOREEEEE!"

"Sha, Georgie, darling," says Mamma. "Don't get so excited."

Pappa is snapping Polaroids. Snapping, waiting, pulling out the film.

I watch the images as the mob of birds turns from tan to black and white.

"Look at that!" says my father. "Some process, huh? A

114

modern miracle! Leon, how's your eye?" he shouts. "Come and look at this! Where's Rebecca? She ought to see this too!"

"Out with Sam," I tell my father.

My sister, Rebecca doesn't do well with commotions. A hundred birds, Rebecca. A thousand. A trillion birds, all from the tri-state area, maybe farther! And right here in Brooklyn! On Crown Street! And in our own back yard! I can just imagine my sister, Rebecca rolling her eyes. I can't imagine her saying, "How interesting! And it's all because of Ruthie's fat collection! Ruthie's amazing fat collection!"

"My God," says my mother. "Look at them all! Leon, is your window closed?"

"Mamma!" exclaims my brother from the bathroom. "It's twenty degrees out there! Why would I have the window open?"

"My God," Mamma is saying, holding Georgie, hurrying from room to room, checking the windows. Georgie is sucking his two fingers, giggling, bouncing and lurching in her arms. "David!" she shouts from the kitchen. "What about the one in the basement?"

"Huh?" says my father, snapping another picture, frowning over the photographic paper he's pulling carefully out of the camera. "Look at this one!" he's saying as the image of the crowd of birds grows slowly darker. "You'll see, they'll perfect it—then you won't have to wait so long for the picture—"

"David!" my mother shouts again. "Yes?" My father is looking up. "What is it, Miriam?"

"Is the window downstairs closed?" Mamma's voice has an edge to it. She's standing at the door of my room holding Georgie. But my father's attention is on the camera. My mother turns and heads for the living room and the porch room, which is at the far end of the house. I

115

hear Georgie giggling. "Isn't it like the frogs?" he's asking. "MAMMA, ISN'T IT LIKE THE FROGS?!"

"Will you look at that picture?" Pappa is asking Leon and me. None of my friends' parents own Polaroid cameras. None of them have movie cameras either. But Pappa does. "This is the modern age!" he declared when we got our television set, the first family on Crown Street to buy one. "The genius of Man!" he says when we watch Mr. Wizard, a television program about science, or when he tells us about his research for the science article he's writing for the newspaper.

I'm drawing the birds, coloring them in as fast as my hands will move. Even with his camera Pappa notices. "That crow looks like it's really flying!" he says and kisses me.

Leon is back at the window, holding a washcloth over his eye. "Let me look at it," says Pappa putting down the camera. Leon takes off the cloth and my father inspects his eye. "It's all bloodshot," complains Leon. My father frowns. "It just looks irritated—Leon, please be more careful—you only get—"

Leon shoots me a blood-shot glance. We both know what our father is about to say.

"—One pair of eyes!" says my father.

"I know, Pappa," says my brother.

"Will you look at this picture?" says Pappa, holding up one with a mob of starlings edging out three crows. "Look at that shot! Ruthie, they really like that feeder!"

"What's that bird with the crest?" asks Leon, looking at my father's picture.

"It's a cardinal!" I answer, pointing to the encyclopedia. Now Leon looks out the window. "Look at how red it is!" he exclaims.

116

"Just like its picture!" I tell Leon, showing him the page. "It's a male. It says, 'when you sight a male there's always a female nearby—they mate for life—'" I read.

"They do? They mate for life? Birds?" my mother is saying. And now Mamma is pressed to the window glass, looking at the bird feeder. Georgie leans his head on her shoulder, sucking his fingers. "Where is she, I wonder?" my mother is asking quietly.

"Look, Mamma! There she is! See her?" I point. "She looks like the male, she's just brown!" Mamma's eyes look lit up, as if the sky suddenly grew bright after the rain.

"I've never seen a cardinal in our back yard!" declares Leon.

"Maybe it's from New Jersey," I suggest. "It must have smelled the suet!"

"In New Jersey?" says Leon.

"Maybe the wind carries it," I say. Leon looks doubtful. "Maybe word just gets around," I say, shrugging. All I know is that Benny Pitt was right. It could have even come from Connecticut, I'm thinking. Birds from the Tri-State Area—Birds From New York, New Jersey and Connecticut. I'm going over it, wondering which works better as a title for my science project.

"It's red," Georgie is saying. "Look, it's RED!"

"Look, it's trying to squeeze through the crowd of starlings," says my father. "I wish this thing had color film! They're working on it, it won't be long," my father is murmuring.

"Wow, will you look at that?" says Leon. "They love that stuff!"

My God, I think, looking out the window, it really is a jamboree, like the frogs in Georgie's book mobbing the frog pond. I want to say so. I want to shout Jamboree! the way my brother, Georgie does. I pinch my mouth closed. But I feel as if I could fly with that mob of birds. The platform is swaying and jerking on its fence post and there's a bird fight going on over the suet. I should have put out more, should have taken all the suet Benny Pitt offered, and would have if it weren't for my sister, Rebecca. My mind is racing with my fingers, working the pages of the article on birds in the encyclopedia.

Starlings and jays and sparrows. Pigeons, chickadees. I can't look them up fast enough. Two more crows land. The other birds, except for the first three crows, scatter into the air then settle back down again.

"David!" says my mother suddenly remembering. "We'll have a house full of birds! Do I have to go down to the basement to find out if you closed the window?"

"Miriam, I never opened it! It's the dead of winter, for God's sake! Stop worrying and look at what's happening! This is amazing!"

"Cat!" says Georgie, pointing. "Cat!" The Lamont's cat, Geoffrey, is sitting on the fence, his tail twitching like crazy.

"Let me get a shot of that!" cries Pappa. Then the camera runs out of film. "For crying out loud, that's my last shot! Leon, put on some clothes and run down to Kogen's. Get two rolls of Polaroid film!"

"Pappa, it's Sunday," says my brother.

"Oh, for God's sake!" says Pappa. "I knew I should have gotten an extra roll!"

"Who knew we were going to have a—a—bird—jamboree in the back yard?" says Mamma. Leon and I turn to our mother. And now she snorts a crazy sort of laugh. Pappa looks at her as if he's been wakened from a dream. He's quiet for a minute. Then he laughs too. It starts slowly like that. But suddenly my parents are laughing so hard all Leon and Georgie and I can do is watch in surprise. Tears are gathering in the corners of my father's eyes. Mamma is breathless. Each of Leon's eyebrows is moving in a different direction. Clumps of shaving cream are slipping down his cheeks past his chin then dropping onto his chest and undershirt. He's looking from my mother to my father, the dangling tissue paper bouncing with the motion of his head. Then an odd-sounding moan escapes from his throat. Then he's laughing too. He looks at Pappa, then Mamma, then me. Then I start laughing. I put the B encyclopedia down and close it. Georgie is sucking his fingers looking from Mamma to Pappa to Leon to me. "Where's my frog book?" he asks around his fingers. "Maaa-mmmaaaa, my boo-ook!"

"Wh—what?" my mother is trying to say. "It's—it's—on—the—Georgie—it's—" but she's laughing too hard to speak.

"Maa-mmmaaa, I want to read it!" My brother has pulled his fingers from his mouth. But Mamma's eyes are fixed on the birds at the feeder. Suddenly she stops laughing and she looks at me. And she says it. "Ruthie, that's your—suet!" she says, stressing the word 'your.' I look at my mother. She's just looking at me, looking surprised. Then something happens to her face. It feels like it happens in slow motion. It lights up again, and she smiles. And I realize she suddenly understands. And I realize she's proud. And in slow motion I'm smiling at her too.

"MAAA-MAAA I want to REEEEED it! The FROG JAMBOREE! I want to REEEEED!"

My father has taken out his handkerchief and is blowing his nose. My mother has turned back to Georgie.

She's thumping on my little brother's back and bouncing him up and down, swaying him side to side, wiping her eyes with the heel of one hand. Mamma glances over at me. Then my parents look at each other again and start laughing. Pappa's laugh is squealing in his throat. He begins talking Yiddish, a word or two between each spasm of laughter. My mother nods and laughs harder. I take Georgie from her and walk down the hall to his room. I get "Frog Jamboree" from his shelf. Georgie puts his fingers back in his mouth. He leans against me, just holding his book. I set him down. He stands there, The Frog Jamboree in one hand, sucking on two fingers of his other.

When I come back to the window of my room, Leon's mouth looks crooked. He's looking up at the ceiling then down at the floor. Then he looks at me, smiling with all his teeth showing. Pappa has his arm around Mamma. "It's good, Miriam," he says. "It's good for the children. It's science, Miriam. And art! Did you see Ruthie's pictures? Did you see the feeder she built? It's like a sculpture!" Mamma is flushed. She's smiling looking at me and nodding.

Outside the birds have settled down on the plywood platform to seriously eat. Georgie wanders back into my room, holding his frog book by one of its covers. It's bumping along the floor, open.

"Georgie, it's a book," I tell him. "Don't treat it that way!"

Georgie is looking up at my parents. "Birds," says Georgie quietly. "Birds."

Rocks and Birds of Brooklyn

Nine species of birds have come to our back yard in the dead of winter. By Sunday night I've combined them with the birds that fly north when spring comes to New York State, New Jersey and Connecticut, and, of course, Brooklyn, which I've learned about in the encyclopedia.

I've eliminated the idea of using my rubber band ball as a project for the Science Fair. I can't have three science projects. But can I really have two? I'll be the only one. But who ever thought so many birds lived in the Tri-State Area? Right here in Brooklyn, on our very street! That's too surprising and important to just keep to yourself. But a fossil, that isn't just nothing, I'm thinking. I'm having this discussion inside myself, working on a drawing of the cardinal husband and wife, coloring the male red and the female red-brown, when my father comes to my door.

"How are the birds?" he asks.

"Pappa, I have fifteen kinds!"

My father looks at the picture of the cardinals. "My mother—your grandmother, Lily, could draw." Pappa says this softly. "Not just music runs in this family!" He kisses me.

"But, Pappa, now I have too many science projects! No one will have two but me!"

My father looks at me. He's thinking. "You have one extra," he says. "Isn't there something called extra credit?" he asks.

"Extra credit?" I repeat.

"Why not?" asks my father.

I smile. "Why not?" I repeat.

What an idea! I think. Mrs. Roth gives Nina Present extra credit for working ahead in her math book while mostly everyone else is struggling to do the day's homework.

I draw purple finches, robins, cardinals, mocking birds, seagulls, blue jays, starlings, grackles, chickadees, crows, pigeons, sparrows, tufted tit mice, gold finches,

121

Helene Lamont's parakeet, and Ella, Aunt Dorothy's canary.

My aunt was so enthused about the idea of my feeding the birds and drawing them that she went to Benny Pitt's to get suet for Ella and put some at the bottom of Ella's cage. "Did she love it, Ruthie!" Aunt Dorothy told me on the telephone. Ella is named for Ella Fitzgerald, the singer, who my aunt adores.

"Ruthie is gifted," Aunt Dorothy tells my mother when my mother tells her she worries about my collections—the rusty pieces of things I find in the street, the rubber bands, and, of course, the fat.

Aunt Dorothy tries to assure my mother that I'm artistic. She also says this about my other projects. For instance when I sewed together a skirt and blouse I hardly ever wore, curious to see if they would make a dress. It almost worked, but not exactly. The waist seemed a little low and it was longer on one side, and when I shortened it, it just seemed longer on the other. I worked on it until finally it was a little too short to wear, so I wore it in the house after school. This made my mother frown. It made my sister, Rebecca roll her eyes. "We can't even give it away!" said Mamma. But Aunt Dorothy thought my mother should buy me a sewing machine and get me lessons to learn how to use it. "You have a gifted daughter, Miriam, stop worrying. Ruthie's creative!"

"Use your gifts, Ruthie," she tells me. "They'll make you a good life!"

I do a drawing of Ella and look through the pages of bird portraits. They're almost done. I write a report about the suet, and about how Pappa and I dug a hole and put up a platform, like a bird buffet table.

I tell about the way the birds arrived after I almost gave up—how they mobbed the suet feeder and about the way my father took pictures with his Polaroid camera. I even write about the way my little brother, Georgie, called the crowd of birds a bird jamboree.

I entertain the idea of doing some other pictures—say, cartoons of grackles and crows eating from tiny plates, maybe with forks and knives, helping themselves at the bird buffet, then sitting on rocks in my back yard, eating their suet delicately, and talking. They might tell bird jokes, like, why did the chicken cross the road? For instance. Huh? I can imagine one of them asking. To get to the other side!

But it walked! one of the birds, maybe a starling, would say. I can just hear the way all those fliers would be chirping and tweeting their laughter, about a bird that has to walk to cross a road. It would be a bird party. Georgie would like that, I'm thinking.

But I'm wondering how it would go over with the judges, Mr. Schreiber, our principal, and Mrs. Harris, our assistant principal. Considering all this I realize I can't remember ever seeing Mrs. Harris smile, or hearing either one of them laugh. I decide against it. Instead I develop the theme about how I waited and waited and waited until the birds finally came, all of us watching out the window, my little brother screaming about the jamboree.

I put sticky corners on Pappa's Polaroid pictures and paste them into the pages of my bird book. Then there's the title. Birds of Brooklyn, New Jersey and Connecticut? What if some did come from New Jersey or Connecticut? I feel sure that birds communicate across state lines. Benny Pitt thinks they do. Why would he have said they'd come all the way from New Jersey?

Hey, there's candy in Brooklyn, lots of it! The New

York birds might call. Come on over, I imagine them saying in bird language people just don't understand, just thinking they're chirping and tweeting happily and they're really talking about some crazy bird party happening in the Pincus' back yard, and who knows what else?

I don't know. The Tri-State Area sounds like the news, not the title of a science project. I decide to use "Bird Buffet," as my title, and not open the question of location beyond the back yard. I letter it in silver crayon on the front cover.

Tuesday night I make a sign, "Rocks and Birds of Brooklyn," using all the colors of my crayon pack. Wednesday, Pappa drives me, my rock collection and my bird book to school. We unload at the gym door. Long tables are filling up with science projects. Aylene has sprouted lima beans in three sour pickle jars. Pappa and I look at each other. He holds up two fingers and winks. "Two science projects for Ruthie Pincus," he whispers and kisses me.

Timmy, Stuie Slatsky's baby Boa Constrictor, is glaring out of his glass tank, his tongue flicking. David Mendelsohn has made a recording thermometer. "Look at that," murmurs my father. "A bimetal strip. It's made of two metals, Ruthie, copper and tin. Each expands and contracts at a different rate as the temperature changes. That's what makes it bend." "Right," says David. "See the needle at the end, Mr. Pincus?" Pappa nods and smiles. "That's how it draws the line on the temperature graph. It's got a well in it that holds ink," David tells us. "Clever, David," says Pappa, touching David on the shoulder. David's father is a science teacher.

I look at Pappa anxiously as we pass to the next table. He looks at me. His forehead is furrowed.

Then he smiles again. "It's an admirable project, a lot of work," he tells me quietly. "Sugar," he says and just smiles. He stops walking. "That insect wing is something unusual. Imagine finding something so—ancient—in our back yard?" It's the way he says the word ancient that makes me feel alone in the world with my father, alone with his green eyes flashing with excitement behind his thick glasses, alone with his high deep forehead, with his smile and with the way he calls me Sugar. It's what makes me almost not care if I win a prize or not. I smile too. "And wait until they see those Polaroids!" says my father.

We find the table with my name and get our cartons. Just then Mrs. Harris passes. "Hello, Mr. Pincus," she greets my father. She nods to me. Pappa and I set up the rock collection. The two halves of limestone with its imprints of the insect wing is in its white box, sitting on its bed of absorbent cotton. I open Bird Buffet and set up my sign.

Ruthie's Rocks and Birds flashes like a rainbow under the bright gym lights. The two projects fill one whole table.

Pappa and I walk up and down the aisles between the other tables to see the rest of the exhibit. Gerald Spitz has filled a big flour jar with guppies darting around frantically, looking like they're searching for the Atlantic Ocean. There are brine shrimp and butterflies, and two shoeboxes of Evy Mailman's mushrooms.

"Can you eat these?" Pappa asks Evy. "Uh, I'm not sure," says Evy. "They grow out of the cracks in our basement floor when it rains."

Donna has a box full of dead moths she's found on Crown Street around the street lights. They're lined up neatly, and identified with labels. One is big, pink and green. "Wow, I never saw that one. It's spectacular!" I tell Donna. "My brother lent it to me," Donna tells me. "He found it in the country last summer." "Luna Moth," I read.

Donna nods. It was dying on the path to our tent." Donna and I exchange looks of sympathy for the moth. "It's beautiful," I tell her, touching its wing.

"You have two projects, Ruthie," says Donna. "Who ever knew there were so many different birds around here!" she says.

"Who ever knew there were so many different kinds of moths!"

"Poor things," says Donna.

"It's better than white quartz," I say. Donna laughs.

"Most people who live in the city have never seen a Luna Moth!" says my father.

"There's one like it in the museum," says Donna.

"But it's rare to find one," says Pappa. Donna and I look at my father gratefully.

Two

My father sits down in the bleachers with the other parents. I look around, amazed. The gym has been transformed. The place where we practice dances, like the cha cha, the place where we play punchball and basketball is now the fourth grade science fair. My stomach feels like Donna Pukatch's moths. But these are still alive, fluttering around inside me.

I stand next to my sign, "Rocks and Birds of Brooklyn," waiting for the judges, Mr. Schreiber, our Principal, and Mrs. Harris, the Assistant Principal who are making the rounds. They stop at the next table to look at Stuie Slatsky's snake, Timmy. Timmy is coiled in his glass tank. Mrs. Harris is scribbling notes on her clipboard. She nods to Stuie. Mr. Schreiber leans forward and taps the glass of Timmy's tank, just at the place where Timmy's head is resting. "Uh—careful—," says Stuie. "You'll wake him up." "He looks awake to me," says the Principal. "His eyes are open!" Mr. Schreiber withdraws his hand. He glances at Stuie. He looks a little annoyed. Then he turns back to Timmy.

Mr. Schreiber's hands are clasped in front of him. He's still leaning toward Timmy's tank. Then, as if he can't help himself, he reaches out and thumps the glass. Stuie and I look at each other. Suddenly the snake's eyes seem to focus and he shoots out his tongue, waggling it in the Principal's direction. Mr. Schreiber jerks straight, startled. "Told you," says Stuie Slatsky. "He sleeps with his eyes open."

"Uh—that's quite a large garden snake!" Mr. Schreiber says to Mrs. Harris, moving closer to her, away from the tank. Stuie picks up his crayon-lettered sign and turns it to face Mr. Schreiber. Mr. Schreiber squints. "Timmy The Boa Constrictor," he reads out loud. His mouth is set in a smile, the same smile he has when he's talking to parents.

"Oh—uh—B—Boa Constrictor?" he repeats, his voice sounding a little high as it comes to the end of the word, constrictor. He glances at Mrs. Harris and raises his eyebrows. "Is—uh—that top secure?" he asks in that same going-high voice, pointing to the screen that rests on Timmy's tank. Mrs. Harris has stepped behind Mr. Schreiber. She peers around his shoulder.

"Oh, don't worry," Stuie laughs. "He's very gentle. I can put him around my neck, wanna see?"

Mrs. Harris' hand moves up to her mouth. Timmy uncoils a little and lurches in her general direction. The Principal has turned to shield Mrs. Harris with his arm. "Ohhh!" cries Mrs. Harris in a voice I've never heard her use. She steps so far back she knocks into Evy Mailman's mushroom project, upsetting the shoe box, spilling the neat rows of mushrooms and dirt onto the table and on Evy's father's jacket, which is draped over Evy's chair. Stuie has lifted the top of Timmy's tank. "Did we wake you up?" He asks the snake. "Come, on, Boy," he's coaxing, his hand now on the inside of the tank, wiggling his fingers to Timmy. Timmy begins to slide toward Stuie. Mrs. Harris grabs for the table to keep from falling. "Ohhhh!" she cries again. Now Stuie's got his fingers around Timmy and he's hauling him out of the tank.

I can see the whites of Mr. Schreiber's eyes behind his glasses. He's standing, rigid, still a little bent. "Come on," Stuie is saying softly to Timmy who is now half in and half out of his tank. Then Timmy's dangling over the table.

"Now—wait a minute," Mr. Schreiber mutters, putting up his hand as Stuie slides Timmy over his shoulders. Then Timmy seems to settle down, draping himself comfortably on Stuie's neck.

Mrs. Harris seems very pale now. She looks like she'd like to jump on the chair with Mr. Mailman's jacket, like someone in a cartoon who's seen a mouse. Timmy's tongue keeps darting and waggling out of his mouth.

"See?" says Stuie, stroking Timmy, giving him a kiss on the head. "See how gentle he is?" Stuie is looking at us from under his eyebrows. He looks like he's wearing a big collar. A snake collar.

Then I'm thinking, don't snakes eat mice? Hmmm. Then I'm wondering where Stuie gets mice. My stomach contracts. I'm picturing how soft and furry and cute mice are. How Donna Pukatch and I would say, ohhh, how sweet, and how Donna would want to take one home if we found it on the street or in the alley. Does Stuie Slatsky kill mice? I'm wondering, trying not to picture it. I decide

I'll ask Stuie about it later.

But Mr. Mailman is reaching to keep Mrs. Harris from falling backwards. She pulls away as if she's been bitten by Timmy and brushes at the dirt that's clinging to her dress. "I'm—uh—sorry!" she says to Evy, who's set the shoe box straight, and is now scooping earth and mushrooms from the table with both hands, putting the mess back into the box, trying to push the mushrooms into rows again. Evy is looking from her work with the mushrooms to the snake, to her father, to Mrs. Harris. Mr. Mailman's eyes are bolted to Timmy as he takes his jacket from the chair, shakes it and puts it on, clearing his throat. It looks like Evy is trying to smile politely to Mrs. Harris. But by the time Evy's smile gets to her face it looks kind of sour.

Mrs. Harris is flushed. "Excuse me!" she's exclaiming softly to Evy and Evy's father. Her knuckles look white, one hand grasping her clip board, the other her pencil, scribbling notes on her pad while also keeping her eyes on Timmy, when her pencil point breaks off. Mrs. Harris' shoulders sag. "Oh, dear!" says Mr. Schreiber. "Here, use this one," he says, patting his shirt pocket. He hands Mrs. Harris a mechanical pencil. He throws another glance at Timmy. Mr. Schreiber is frowning. His eyes look round, a lot of their whites showing, making them look a little like fried eggs, except the centers are brown. Then he hustles Mrs. Harris on to David Mendelsohn's recording thermometer. I notice that Mrs. Harris still looks a little pale.

I look back at Stuie. He's hoisting Timmy from his neck and settling him back into his tank. "Good boy," Stuie is crooning softly, stroking him. I really want to put my hand in Timmy's tank and stroke him too. I'd like to feel his shiny skin. I'd really like to ask Stuie to let me drape Timmy around my neck too. I can imagine the pleasant feel of his weight on my shoulders. But I just can't get the thought of Stuie Slatsky killing mice out of my head, and I am struggling not to let myself picture it.

Mr. Schreiber and Mrs. Harris have reached David's recording thermometer. They are both bent, reading David's sign. Mr. Schreiber puts his hand to his chin and looks puzzled. "What's a bimetallic strop?" he asks David after a moment.

"It's strip, not strop," says David. "My fountain pen leaks."

"Strip?" the Principal repeats.

"A bimetal strip," says David. One side expands, the other contracts—with heat or cold.

"Oh—uh huh!" says Mr. Schreiber.

Mrs. Harris is making notes on her pad with Mr. Schreiber's mechanical pencil. She still looks a little pale. "Look at that odd line it's drawing," she says quietly.

"Um hum," answers David. "See it going down?"

"Uh-huh?" says Mrs. Harris.

"That means the temperature is dropping," says David.

"In here?" asks Mr. Schreiber.

"Right," answers David.

"I wonder why that would be," says the Principal.

"Well that happens in winter," says David. "When the furnace cycles off. Then the furnace thermostat signals the furnace to go on again—and the line goes back up as it warms up."

Mr. Schreiber's eyes are following David's finger, tracing the curves of the line printing on the slowly spinning drum of David's recording thermometer. Mrs. Harris is nodding, taking notes.

"Ye—es," says Mr. Schreiber. "I know that!"

"It—it's pretty," says Mrs. Harris. "As if someone

drew mountains, look...now it's dipping lower than the other—well—valleys...lovely, really," she says, smiling. I see her teeth, realizing I've never noticed them before, never noticed there's a gap between the top two, the kind you could whistle through. After Stuie's snake, she really doesn't seem herself. David is smiling too, nodding. "That means it's getting colder and colder. Maybe the furnace is broken."

"Broken?" Mr. Schreiber repeats. He straightens up. "Bill!" He calls suddenly, looking around for the janitor. He hurries toward the door of the gym. Mrs. Harris looks after him then starts toward me. I'm standing in front of my rocks and birds. I move out of the way so she can read the sign.

"Rocks and Birds of Brooklyn," reads Mrs. Harris, making a note just as the fire bell starts clanging. Mr. Schreiber is at the thermostat, which hangs on the wall near the double doors of the gym. He looks upset. Next to the thermostat is the fire alarm. "Darn! I didn't mean to set that off!" he calls. "I'm just trying to—turn up this—heat!" he says, fumbling around with the alarm and turning the dial on the thermostat, both at the same time.

"Noooo-oo!" Mr. Schreiber is saying next, first to the alarm, then to the crowd in the gym. "Noooo!" waving his arms. Students, teachers and parents are looking around. A few have begun to hurry toward Mr. Schreiber and the door. In rushes Bill, the janitor. "Can you do something about this?" the Principal is shouting over the clanging alarm.

Bill looks angry. "Darn kids!" Bill shouts to Mr. Schreiber.

"Fire drill!" calls Mr. Stern, one of the fourth grade teachers.

"Noooo!" Mr. Schreiber is calling, waving his hands at

Mr. Stern. Mrs. Harris looks dazed, two fingers pressing into her cheek, making two indentations so her face looks lopsided.

"Which one of you set that thing off?" Bill is demanding, looking around, as Mr. Schreiber reaches the stage. "Attention!" cries the Principal, setting off a whine in the sound system. "Let's, uh, settle down!" he's calling to the crowd, which has begun to form into classes, lining up in front of their teachers.

Bill is turning something in the box that holds the fire alarm and suddenly the clanging stops. "Who pulled that thing?" fumes Bill.

"May I have your attention...!" shouts Mr. Schreiber into the microphone. "Is that a siren? Is it the Fire Department?" he asks the air.

"It's the darned mike!" says Bill. "You'd better stop shouting into it!" he tells the Principal. But Mr. Schreiber can't hear him over the microphone's wail. "Oh, for Heaven's sake!" says the Principal. "It's the fire truck. Now the Fire Department's involved!"

Bill hurries over and takes hold of the microphone and shuts it off. Everyone stops like a game of freeze tag. Mr. Schreiber talks quietly to Bill, who is scowling. Bill crosses the gym to the thermostat, looks at the Principal and shrugs. "Looks fine to me," calls Bill.

"Hey, look!" calls David Mendelsohn. "The line's going back up!"

Maxine Farrell and Joey Shapiro start chasing each other around the gym, zigzagging through the crowd.

"Please stop that running!" Mrs. Roth is calling. It's ten minutes to three when Mr. Schreiber finally joins Mrs. Harris, who's looking through the pages of my bird book, a smile playing about her mouth. The Principal takes out his handkerchief, mops his forehead and sighs. Then he looks at my sign. "Rocks and Birds of Brooklyn," he reads, sounding a little distracted. But when he sees the insect wing he bends to look more closely. "My goodness, isn't that a fossil?"

I nod and feel myself flush with pride.

Mrs. Harris has lifted her glasses and is examining Pappa's Polaroid picture on the cover of my bird book. "Where did you find so many birds?" she asks.

"It was the suet," I tell her.

"The what?" she asks.

"We put it in the back yard and they came—Benny Pitt says it's like bird candy."

"Benny who?" asks the Assistant Principal.

"Pitt," I answer. "The kosher butcher on Troy Avenue, it's in my report."

Mrs. Harris looks blank. She turns back to the bird book and opens to my report. Then she looks at it closely. "The N's are all handwritten!" she says.

"The N key doesn't work," I answer.

"My R's have stopped working," confides Mrs. Harris, and there's that smile again. The space between her teeth makes her look suddenly pretty.

"I used to collect rocks," says Mr. Schreiber looking first at me and then at Mrs. Harris. "I always hoped to find a fossil. Where did you get this, at the museum?" He's leaning toward me with his thick, gray eyebrows raised above his glasses.

"In the back yard," I answer. "When my father and I were putting up the bird feeder."

"Really?" says the Principal. "I've never seen one like it!" And now he's looking at it very carefully. "It looks like a dragon fly wing!"

I'm nodding, smiling.

"Rocks and Birds of Brooklyn," he reads again. "Two

science projects!" says Mr. Schreiber.

"I couldn't decide," I answer.

"Two!" repeats Mrs. Harris, looking pleased. Then Mr. Schreiber and Mrs. Harris look at each other. Mrs. Harris writes with Mr. Schreiber's mechanical pencil on her clip board.

While we're waiting for the prizes to be announced I confront Stuie Slatsky. "So what do you feed him?" I ask, and I know my voice is a little loud.

"Huh? Who?" asks Stuie, looking at me.

"Timmy? What do you feed him?" My hands are clenched and I am hoping Stuie will say something like, oh, cornflakes and bananas, or maybe, meatballs and spaghetti.

"Huh?" Stuie asks. "Oh, mice, sometimes rats," he answers.

I swallow. "Where—where do you get them, Stuie?" I ask. "Huh? Oh, we buy them at the pet store," answers Stuie. "You look funny."

"Then you kill them? Then you kill them, Stuie? You kill mice and rats?" My voice is rising.

"We buy them frozen," Stuie answers. "Your face looks funny," he says again. Stuie's mouth is twisted and he's frowning. I'm thinking his face looks funny too. "My father feeds Timmy," he's saying, looking over at his snake. "I wish he'd just eat dog food," he says, sighing.

I take a breath and swallow. I put my hand over my mouth and squeeze my lips tight.

"Your face looks so funny," Stuie is saying. I'm nodding and pointing to him wanting to tell him that his skin looks clammy, like Timmy's. But now Stuie's opened Timmy's tank. He's stroking the snake's glossy, scaly skin. And suddenly I feel an odd feeling in my stomach, a kind of queasy relief and giddiness that makes me want to laugh, but my eyes are tearing up at the same time. Suddenly I realize I admire Stuie Slatsky.

I look toward the stage and see Mrs. Harris. She looks back at me and I see her flash that space between her teeth.

The Prize

"Testing...testing...," says Mr. Schreiber quietly, looking suspiciously at the microphone. "May I have your attention please!" Mrs. Harris plays three notes on her chime. The gym falls silent. Everyone is waiting. But Pappa stands up and makes his way from the bleacher seats to my table. Then Mrs. Harris tells us we've all done a good job on our science projects. She tells us she's proud to be the assistant principal of Public School Two-Twenty-One.

Mr. Schreiber is patting his jacket pockets. He doesn't find what he's looking for. Next he pokes his hand inside his jacket, and searches his shirt pocket. Next the pockets of his pants. He's beginning to scowl, his thick gray eyebrows are pulled together at the top of his nose.

Mrs. Harris doesn't seem to notice. She still seems different than usual. Ordinarily her face doesn't move much. But since Stuie's snake waggled his tongue at her she looks a little dreamy. Now she's looking around the gym at us all, really looking, and the corners of her mouth are turned up.

"Where is that thing?!" Mr. Schreiber says a little irritably into the microphone. It begins to hum. This attracts Mrs. Harris' attention. She puts her hand over the microphone and the humming stops. "I've lost that paper!" Mr. Schreiber tells Mrs. Harris. Now he looks a

135

little helpless. Mrs. Harris hands him her clipboard, whispers to him and points to the top sheet of paper. Then she looks back out at us all and smiles.

"Oh, um hum!" says the principal. "Now let's see..."

I glance at my father. His eyes meet mine, bright with expectation.

"Here it comes," I whisper. My father nods.

Mr. Schreiber is clearing his throat. "...Honorable mention goes to...George Goldfarb for his brine shrimp." Now Mr. Schreiber is shuffling through the pages of Mrs. Harris' clipboard. She takes it from his hands and pulls out several sheets of paper. I can see the heavy black print of the awards certificates. Then she hands one to George Goldfarb who's come up to the stage to collect it. There is some polite applause and Mr. Schreiber smiles at George, that same smile he smiles at parents, the way he smiled at Stuie Slatsky when he discovered Stuie's snake was a boa constrictor.

"Third prize," says the principal next, "goes to...Tim—uh—that's Stuart Slatsky, for his Boa—for his snake." Stuie scoops Timmy out of his tank and holds him up for everyone to see. Timmy's coiling and lurching, flopping against Stuie. Then he slithers against Stuie's chest and wraps himself around his arm, making his way to Stuie's neck as Stuie hurries to the front of the gym.

A few people gasp. Someone's mother hurries out of the gym carrying a small child and the door closes with a squeal. As Stuie approaches the stage, Mr. Schreiber steps back. He's leaning to one side, away from Stuie and Timmy, and Mrs. Harris has stepped behind him again. Stuie's got one hand on Timmy. With the other he accepts his award certificate which Mrs. Harris is holding by its corner, dangling it at Stuie past Mr. Schreiber's arm. Only a few people are clapping. There's a lot of murmuring and

136

some laughter.

"It's a Boa—look!" Barbara Goldstein's little brother, Harvey, is shouting. He gallops to the front of the gym. "A Boa, a Boa Constrictor! Look!" shouts Harvey.

"Harvey!" calls Barbara's mother, hurrying forward. "Don't get too close!"

"It's a real Boa Constrictor!" shouts Harvey again, and now he's jumping up and down.

Mrs. Goldstein picks up Harvey and hurries with him back to their seats. She looks upset.

"Let's settle down," says the principal as Stuie and Timmy make their way back to their table.

"Thank you, Stuart," says Mr. Schreiber. "Better put that thing—uh—that Boa—uh—your snake—away!" His voice is just a little loud and the microphone starts to whine again. Mr. Schreiber jiggles it. The siren gets louder. Now Mrs. Harris looks annoyed. She pulls the microphone toward her and switches it off then on again, which takes care of the problem.

I turn to Pappa. He looks at me and smiles.

"Can everyone hear me?" Mr. Schreiber is calling.

"Ye-ess!" some people call back.

Mr. Schreiber clears his throat. "Second prize..." he says, finding his place on the clipboard. I look anxiously at Pappa who's now looking anxiously at Mr. Schreiber. "—Goes to David Mendelsohn, for his recording thermometer!" There's a sinking feeling in my stomach. Second prize for metal that expands and contracts with the temperature? I'm thinking. I look at the table with my birds and rocks. They're only from the back yard, I think—and the butcher shop. I pinch my mouth shut and try to imagine how I'll feel gathering them back up again, carrying them to the car with my father. I think of those black printed prize certificates, none with my name.

Across the gym Mrs. Roth is looking over at David

Mendelsohn and smiling. She looks proud. I watch as she turns her head toward my father. Aylene Muntzer is directly in my line of vision. As I watch Mrs. Roth I shift my gaze toward Aylene and wonder vaguely why Aylene's green eyes, which usually look so slitty, look so wide.

"Ruthie!" my father is saying. His arm is around my shoulders and he's shaking me. "Ruthie, you've won first prize!"

"—For her rare fossil and rock collection!" Mr. Schreiber is announcing. People are applauding. Pappa's face is lit up. "And—and—" the principal is calling. Mrs. Harris begins to play her chimes. "And a very special award for extra credit goes to Ruthie Pincus for her art and photographic documentation and report about birds!"

My head feels light, as if it's not really attached, as if it's floating to the ceiling of the gym like a helium balloon. As I turn from my father to Mr. Schreiber, Aylene's face passes, then Joannie Nevins'. Their eyes, locked on to each other's, look like they're popping.

"Two awards to one person?" I hear Evy say to her father.

"Two awards to one person!" exclaims Mrs. Harris playing the chimes excitedly.

"How unusual," says Evy's father looking at me, smiling crooked the way Evy does.

Two two two two, I'm saying inside as my feet dance across the polished wooden boards of the floor on my way to the front of the gym. Two two two! As Mrs. Harris hands me the two pieces of paper with my name on them. I see the space between her teeth peeking out under her top lip and hear a sound which I realize is a giggle. A giggle coming from Mrs. Harris! Two two two two two!

"Congratulations," says David Mendelsohn's father nodding to my two prize certificates rippling as I pass David's table. He and David are packing up the recording thermometer. David smiles. I pinch my lips together. "You found a rare fossil," he says quietly. He waves his second prize certificate and punches me in the shoulder. I punch him back. I can't really believe what's happened.

Mrs. Roth hugs me. Donna rushes up to my table. I look at her and I see she's happy for me. "You look like a zombie!" she says. She puts her hands on both my shoulders and shakes me. Then we begin jumping up and down laughing.

Everyone's begun to pack up. Mr. Stern and Bill are folding up tables and chairs. The gym is beginning to look like itself. Pappa and I pack away my trays of rocks. "We'll make two trips," says my father. "I'll bring around the car." I pass Stuie as he's covering Timmy's tank with a blanket. "Did you ever try cat food?" I ask. Stuie nods. "He won't even smell it," he says. Then he puts out his hand and we shake. "Congratulations," we say at the same time and laugh.

"Extra credit!" says Pappa, laughing, as we carry our cartons to the car. I go back for the last box and the bird album. Joannie Nevins, Evy and Aylene are looking at the Polaroid pictures of the mob of birds. "Look at all of them!" Evy is saying. "What's that they're diving for?" asks Joannie. "What do you think they're diving for?" snaps Aylene. "Birdseed!"

"Fat!" I answer and they look up. Evy puts down the book. I pick it up.

"Fat?" repeats Joannie.

"An award for fat?" says Aylene as I put the book in its carton.

"The birds love it," I say without looking at them.

"Suet from the butcher shop. It's like bird candy."

"Not when it turns rotten," says Aylene.

"Then it's even better," I say, sliding my two awards toward me across the table, loving the sound. "Then it's like aged cheese—like—cheddar, or gorgonzola," I say.

"Gorgonzola?" repeats Joannie.

"What's gorgonzola?" says Evy Mailman.

"Cheese," says Mr. Mailman. "Let's go, Evy."

When I reach the door and see Pappa waving from the car window I look quickly over my shoulder. Joannie, Aylene and Evy are still turned toward me. Aylene looks sour. Joannie's mouth is open. Evy is smiling her crooked smile.

BOOK FOUR

The Beauty of Mamma's Singing

"Eat, Rosie," I hear my Aunt Dorothy tell Aunt Rose, my three aunts and Pappa sitting at the kitchen table talking quietly, lingering over supper.

They're still talking when I say good night. Aunt Rose hugs me. Her skin is pale, but her eyes are bright. There's something serious in her face, a line between her eyebrows that seems new.

From the doorway of my room I can see the worry on Mamma's face after my aunts leave. "She's had a hard time," I hear Pappa say quietly.

Aunt Rose is home from the hospital. After a few weeks she goes back to her job keeping the books for a department store on Atlantic Avenue. She travels by subway as she always did. The family worries. Her piano stays covered with its brocade cloth. But after another few weeks she begins to play it again.

When my mother washes dishes she sings my Aunt's name. My mother is praying. She says, God, God, God. Thank you. Thank you thank you thank you thank you. Then my mother just takes off in her operatic voice. I don't think anyone would understand Mamma's singing, her mix of Yiddish and English, Italian- and French- sounding gibberish—but us—Pappa, Leon, Rebecca and me. It's part of the life of our house on Crown Street, when dinner is finished and my little brother, Georgie, is asleep. When Rebecca and I have cleared the table, and my father is in his office, writing for his newspaper, and Leon and Rebecca and I are

141

doing our homework, and the house is quiet. Mamma washes the dishes and scrubs the kitchen, praying and singing this way.

And now my mother's singing is beautiful, filling the kitchen, overflowing down the hall into all the rooms of the house, thanking God that Aunt Rose is well again.

Sometimes my Aunt Rose takes Rebecca and me out on a Saturday or Sunday afternoon. We go to the zoo at Prospect Park. Or we just walk up Utica Avenue, looking into shop windows. We stop at the nickel machine and buy Indian Nuts. When I try to separate the delicate nut meats from their shells they splinter and mash together. But Aunt Rose splits them with one perfect snap between her crooked front teeth. She gives one to my sister and one to me. Another to my sister, another to me, as we walk back to Crown Street, the daylight fading into dusk, the three of us telling jokes and giggling, Aunt Rose calling us Becky and Rudy.

Piano Lessons

My mother and father have bought a piano. It sits in our living room, its ebony finish sleek and dark. It looks like the one that is our Aunt Rose's, on Carroll Street, where Aunt Rose lives with our grandmother. But this one is smaller.

"A Baby Grand!" says our mother. "A Steinway! Imagine!" she exclaims. But she looks worried. "Be very gentle with it," she tells my sister, Rebecca, and me. "It's a delicate instrument." Then Mamma turns back to the dough she's mixing for kreplach, or continues tucking our brother, Georgie's shirt into his pants, or she scrubs harder at the kitchen floor she's washing. "It's the most valuable thing we've ever owned." This last thing she says quietly, to herself.

Pappa and Mamma have saved for two years, put aside money that could have been used for a new washing machine, to replace the one that knocks when it agitates, and which Pappa has to bolt and wire together every so often so that Mamma can turn the wringer, while she talks to God about Georgie's tantrums, or Rebecca's and my arguments, asking what she has done to deserve children like these. Or it could have been used to buy a new couch to replace the old red and white flowered couch that sags and is threadbare at the arm rests and which Mamma keeps covered with bedspreads. It belonged to Pappa's mother, my grandmother Lily, who died before I was born. But my father wants my sister and me to study the piano.

"Music," says Pappa. "Is in the family." He says this in a voice that is soft, and hushed, and sometimes even sounds like music, the deep, wavery notes of the symphonies he plays on the phonograph. "Music is an inheritance that would be a sin to squander," Pappa tells my sister Rebecca and me. "And we have a piano teacher in the family who has performed at Carnegie Hall! This is a rare and wonderful thing." Says my father. "A great gift!" Mamma's sister, our Aunt Rose, is a classical pianist.

Aunt Rose comes every Saturday afternoon to teach us the piano. An hour's lesson each for Rebecca and then me. Aunt Rose and my mother call our Steinway a pyahh-no, using a careful and exotic English that is different than the way everyone else in Brooklyn speaks.

Uncle Ben, Mamma's brother, laughs at the way my

mother and aunt speak. He says they sound like actresses, or like they grew up in England. But Pappa says they speak that way because they are cultured. Because they've been raised with music and with art. Prints of Renoir's Young Girl at the Piano and Degas' dancers hang on the walls around Aunt Rose's piano on Carroll Street. Prints of Van Gogh's Sunflowers and his Bridge at Arles hang over our red-flowered couch.

After the first few weeks of piano lessons, the printed music sheets of black marks and lines begin to mean sounds. Middle C has a line through it and looks like Saturn with its ring. Rebecca and I learn the scales and practice all week between lessons.

When my aunt plays the scales they sound light and beautiful, not like scales but like a melody. Her hands play each note differently, sometimes striking its key sharply, sometimes hardly seeming to touch another. Her arms rise, lifting into the air above the keys like ballet dancers, hands like birds. She looks now at the keys, now at me, raises her head looking past the piano as she listens to the sounds of the notes she's playing. Her face is first intent, then soft. When she finishes the scales she turns to me and smiles, and her crooked teeth have a way they look, like the notes sound, like the trilling, up-and-down melody of the scales. Our Aunt Rose plays at all the family gatherings. She has played in concert with great musicians, people who visit America from Europe to perform.

During the week I practice my scales and imagine my aunt coming Saturday, sitting next to me, nodding and smiling as I play. Unlike my sister, Rebecca, whose fingers are long and slender, my fingers, short and blunt, stumble over the notes. I practice and practice so the notes will sound smooth. Practice and practice and practice, crossing my thumb under my third finger on the way up the key board, stretching my third finger over my thumb on the way down, imagining my aunt's smile of pleasure at my hard work. "Good, Rudy!" Aunt Rose says inside me. She is the only one who calls me that name, as she is the only one that calls my sister "Becky."

There are times I forget that I am practicing scales, and play their notes, listening, stretching my legs to touch the pedals, savoring the amplified, lengthened tones. Then for a moment I feel as if Aunt Rose and I are one person.

Before the year is over Rebecca is working on Beethoven's "Für Elise." I am working on Mozart's "Turkish March." I listen to Rebecca's lesson from my room, waiting until two o'clock, when my turn will come to sit with Aunt Rose. I listen as my aunt plays Beethoven's notes like a dancing river, rushing and bubbling over stones in the sunlight. Then Rebecca plays the passage she's learning, slowly, stopping and starting.

"Good, Becky!" I hear my aunt tell my sister. "Sing it! Sing the notes, it will help you learn," I hear her say. I draw or do my homework, or play with Hannah, my doll, listening while my aunt plays another passage. Then Rebecca tries, slowly, long silences between notes. Then she plays it again, and again, until it begins to sound like music.

"It just needs practice," I hear Aunt Rose say.

Then it's my turn.

I play the scales. My aunt listens. I play them slowly so I won't stumble.

"Good!" says my aunt, and sometimes, "Lovely!" Then my heart feels warm, and I think that all I want to do is spend hours practicing, to hear her say lovely! again; or to feel her put her arm around me and squeeze my shoulders and laugh with pleasure in her high-pitched voice.

Aunt Rose's fingers are also long and slender. But they're delicate like my mother's and Aunt Dorothy's. My hands are square like Pappa's. My fingers struggle over the notes of the "Turkish March." Aunt Rose plays the first phrase. She sings its five notes, la la la, la la! "Sing it first, Ruthela," she tells me. We sing those five notes together, but when I try to play them I strike two keys instead of one.

"Try it again," says my aunt.

I hold my hands, fingers extended, next to hers. "My hands are fat," I say.

My aunt looks at me. She takes my hands between hers. Her hands are warm. "They're earthy hands. Artists' hands, Rudy," she tells me. "Here, listen..." Then she plays the whole piece, so I can hear how the passages fit together. "Beethoven had strong, broad fingers like yours," she says.

Sometimes I hear Mamma singing Mozart's melody, in her beautiful, crazy, French and Italian opera. *Nee-la-to-la tay-um-pwwah!* sings my mother in the kitchen, two rooms away, as my aunt and I play.

It is true that my mother's family is full of music. My grandfather sometimes sits up in his sleep and conducts, as if there were a symphony orchestra in his room, right there with my grandmother snoring next to him, her teeth in a glass on her night table. Sometimes he sings and it wakes my grandmother. "Sam! What are you doing? Wake up!" my grandmother tells him. "'Sam! You're dreaming!' I have to shake him!" she tells us.

My grandmother's father was a scholar. He studied Torah, the holy books, and the writings of the great rabbis. But my grandfather's family went to hear the symphonies that were performed in the concert halls in St. Petersburg, in Russia. "Your grandfather's family was cultured!" Mamma tells us. "Your grandfather knows the great Toscanini!"

146

Uncle Ben laughs when the family talks about the way my grandfather conducts in his sleep. But Mamma doesn't laugh, neither does Aunt Dorothy or Aunt Rose. It's his deep love of music, one or the other says. Then my father nods with satisfaction. It's in the family, he says, looking from my sister to me. A gift that must not be squandered!

Rebecca practices every day. Her eyes move from the sheet music to the ivory keys and ebony wood sharps. But between lessons, the hour I sit at the Steinway to practice moves slowly by. The black music notations for Mozart's Turkish March swim across their lines as my fingers fall short of the notes and play two together, souring the melody. I don't know how I'll ever learn it. I lose my place, bang on the keys.

"Ruthie!" shouts my mother, from the doorway of the kitchen, calling across the dining room to the living room, the piano room. "What are you doing?!"

"I'm sorry, Mamma!" I say.

"That piahh-no cost a fortune! It's a delicate instrument, Ruthie!"

I can hear Pappa telling us again that music runs in Mamma's family—a gift that must not be thrown away, not be arois gevorfen—thrown out the window! But without Aunt Rose sitting next to me it is hard to sit on the piano bench for an hour to practice. When my mother doesn't remind me I forget.

We spend weeks on Mozart's Turkish March, my fingers playing too fast, jumbling notes. Playing too slowly, stopping, starting, my left hand losing my right hand's place, until my aunt thinks we should try something else.

"Beethoven." She announces one day. She smiles as if she's sharing a secret.

147

My heart rises. When I hear my aunt play *Für Elise* during my sister's lesson, its notes so haunting and beautiful, I stop what I'm doing to listen at the door of the dining room. I stay at the doorway while Rebecca plays Beethoven's melody, over and over again, until it sounds smooth—not like the sweet river that pulls at my throat when Aunt Rose plays, but, well, lovely.

The following Saturday Aunt Rose takes a new piece of sheet music out of her bag. Printed across the cover is the name, Ludwig Von Beethoven, then, *The Moonlight Sonata*. "Listen to it, Ruthela," says my aunt. "It's so very beautiful."

As she plays she closes her eyes. She sways forward and back, side to side. Her lips part in a smile and show her crooked teeth. Like Mamma and Aunt Dorothy, Aunt Rose is beautiful. "Three beautiful daughters God gave me," says my grandmother. "And a son as handsome as a movie star. More handsome!" Aunt Rose is the youngest of the four.

Aunt Rose plays the sad and beautiful notes of the *Moonlight Sonata* until the last note rests on the air, then vanishes as she releases the pedal. A tear spills over onto her cheek. She wipes it away with a finger, laughs, then kisses me. I smile back at her, thinking, I don't know how I'll ever learn it, but I know I will try if it takes me all my life.

"We'll do it in small pieces, Rudy—just the first movement. When you're older we'll work on the whole piece."

Grandpa Sam

One Friday I hurry up Troy Avenue before Aylene and

Joannie leave the school yard. When I get home I use my key. No one is home. Mamma is helping my grandmother on Carroll Street. Georgie is at Aunt Dorothy's. Grandpa Sam is sick.

Mamma has gone to read to him from his newspaper. Mamma's pot roast is on the stove. There's a note on the kitchen counter. "Set the table, Ruthie. I'll be home by 4."

On Saturday Aunt Dorothy calls. She tells my mother that my grandfather can't get out of bed. I see my mother's face as she tells this to me. My mother looks small and curled up as she struggles into her coat to hurry over to Carroll Street. Aunt Rose comes in the afternoon to give Rebecca and me our piano lessons. I listen as Rebecca works on *Für Elise*. Then Aunt Rose and I work on *The Moonlight Sonata*. Mamma comes in as we finish. Then Mamma and Aunt Rose talk softly in the kitchen, Mamma washing dishes, Aunt Rose drying them. They speak in Yiddish.

The Pantry

Wednesday, after dinner, Mamma, Aunt Dorothy and Aunt Rose are standing in the shadows of the pantry, the tiny room next to the kitchen. I'm walking up the hall to hear what they're saying, to hear why they sound the way they do. My God, Aunt Dorothy says, holding up a glass tube that looks like it belongs to David Mendelsohn's chemistry set. She's holding it toward the light filtering in through the opening under the cabinets that join the pantry to the kitchen. Through that opening you can pass ketchup and mustard to the kitchen from the pantry shelves, you can put on puppet shows, you can call

149

to Georgie then duck, if you want to confuse my little brother. We have to get him to the hospital! Aunt Dorothy is saying now.

Mamma and Aunt Rose are smaller than Aunt Dorothy who is tall. The three sisters move like birds, in jumps, blinking, looking at the test tube, looking at each other, the floor, the ceiling, at Aunt Dorothy. They are puppets. They are shadows. They are silhouettes on the electric wires along the street. Silhouettes in bird movement, making the wires bounce in that dark pantry with the light filtering into it from the kitchen like a distant sun lighting up the yellow fluid in the tube turning turquoise blue as we all watch it like some strange magic in a movie.

My brother Leon comes to the doorway of his room. He walks up the hall to where I'm standing and pulls me by the hand, pulls me into his room, far away from the doorway, into the corner where the dark wood wardrobe stands. "Grandpa is sick, Ruthie," he's telling me, looking at me, looking away. He holds onto my hand. His hand feels cold. "Grandpa—his legs—he can't walk anymore." I'm thinking that my grandfather has his cane. Why can't he walk the way he always does, leaning on his cane?

"His legs," my brother says again.

His legs? I'm asking my brother. What, Leon, what? Leon's face looks so odd, and the words I'm asking him are sounds inside my chest that won't come up where Leon would be able to hear them. What is that thing, turquoise blue, I want to ask. But Leon knows my question. "They're measuring his blood sugar," he's telling me. That's what Mamma and Aunt Dorothy and Aunt Rose are doing with that glass tube. My eyes are two mouths of questions, asking what I have no words for. Diabetes, says my brother. My grandfather has diabetes. "They have to take off his legs," he then says.

"What?" I finally cry out loud. But it feels like a dream.

Leon's eyes and nose, his mouth and chin look like there is too much space between them. But his blue eyes, the color of my grandmother's, hold onto mine. Then he's pulling me close, his arms closing around me and I feel him shudder. "They have to—amputate his legs," my brother is murmuring. And when he holds me away from him to look at me again he's clutching my hands and his face is wet and crumpled.

How do you take legs off? How? I'm thinking. You take legs off a plastic Cracker Jack toy that snaps together, but not from a person! These thoughts are racing through me. Then something cold moves through the center of me. I look at my brother, Leon. He looks far away. The air in his room sounds like water rushing through my ears.

Then I know. This is Death. And though I know that such a thing exists, away from us, outside somewhere, far away from the people I know, I feel myself go hard like the concrete sidewalk, like the row of steps in front of our house. Because I know that that thing that had nothing to do with the Pincuses has arrived, has walked up those steps, where I play stoop ball, and is standing in the midst of us now. It's here, on Crown Street, and around the corner at Aunt Dorothy's on Montgomery Street. It's three blocks away on Carroll Street at my grandmother's and grandfather's and Aunt Rose's house. It's in the pantry, in the shadowy forms of my aunts and that glass tube glowing like some blue-green diamond. It's Death.

Death has come here. It's around my brother, Leon, and it's around me. It makes the air of Leon's room smell foul, like something that's been too long in the refrigerator. Like a dead cat in the gutter. The air is so

151

putrid with it that it's hard to breathe. There's a fish that's been thrown away, thrown right onto our stoop, right next to our porch, and it's turning black, and a cloud is rising from its sad little broken body, and the cloud is covering our house. The smell is seeping under our front door, closed so tight against it. Locked and bolted against it. Death. And no one can send it away.

And I hold onto my brother, Leon, and he holds onto me. And we cry one cry.

Smiling

The days pass and my parents, my aunts and uncles go to the hospital to sit with my grandfather and stay with my grandmother so that she isn't alone. On the telephone my mother speaks in Yiddish. At night her crying is a terrible sound through the wall of my bedroom. Pappa says her name, *Miriam, Miriam*. I am afraid.

Then one afternoon Rebecca and I are eating supper at the kitchen table. Pappa is at night school. Mamma is serving us from a plate of spaghetti and string beans. We are eating salad. I look at my mother and forget that I'm eating. Her face is small and sad and white. I feel my own face, the inside of my mouth. I feel my teeth. They are chewing something, maybe paper. Died, she is whispering about our grandfather. Grandpa Sam has died.

I can't make sense of this word, can't connect what my mother has said to my grandfather. It glares in the overhead light fixture, sounds with the refrigerator motor as if there were cotton stuffed in my ears.

An odd smile is pulling at Rebecca's mouth. Rebecca's face is moving slowly, like it doesn't know what to do, the same way my ears don't know what to do with the word Mamma has spoken.

I see my grandfather's face, his mouth serious, his white eyebrows bushy, his chin stubbled with white, unshaven beard. His cane. How can this word, this thing be true? My sister Rebecca's face is twisting in slow motion into this crazy smile and Mamma stands there holding a plate of spaghetti and string beans, looking at us with her brown eyes that say they can't understand the word she's using either. Not about our grandfather. Not about her father.

In that strange hollow air, the tunnel that is our kitchen, I dimly know that my mother understands that Rebecca's crazy smile is her crying.

Because I know. I know Rebecca is crying so hard and deep that her eyes can't make tears and her face just twists that way instead.

Aunt Irene

Aunt Irene Levine wears red lipstick. Her hair is black, pinned up in two rolls, one behind each ear. She wears tortoise shell barrettes. She wears beaded dresses, and when she laughs her red lipstick becomes a big laughing red oval around her teeth. She plays cards, and you can hear her voice when everyone else is talking. She smokes cigarettes. Her husband, named Sam like our grandfather, smokes cigars.

Aunt Irene isn't really our aunt. She's Aunt Dorothy's best friend, and close to our family. She comes to stay with Georgie and me because Pappa says we're too young to go to the cemetery where they are burying my grandfather. She isn't wearing lipstick now, and she isn't laughing. Her smile is sweet and her voice is soft as she and Georgie and me play jacks. And she reads to Georgie from the book she's brought him called, "Reptiles."

I'm trying to tell Georgie about snakes, but Georgie just wants to look at the frogs. So we do. And even though we talk softly and smile, and even though we're here in Georgie's room and my parents and family are at the cemetery where we are too young to go, I know now. I know about death. I know that it makes people, even Aunt Irene, look soft and sweet and sad. And it touches Georgie, who talks softly too, his brown eyes looking into our faces.

And it sits in me like a stone.

Carroll Street

Mamma and I go to Carroll Street where only Aunt Rose and my grandmother are now. I keep looking for my grandfather, think I see his shadow move in the doorway. I turn my head, but he isn't there. His cane leans against his big, blue upholstered chair. The cushion is carved, creased with his weight, as if he had just stood up to go into the kitchen after reading his newspaper, to drink a glass of tea.

Aunt Rose sits at the piano playing the music of Franz Liszt. The Liszt book is open on the music rest. She presses her cheek against mine when I sit down on the piano bench, to be close to her. She doesn't turn her head to see me. She just plays. Her eyes are closed because she doesn't need the sheet music to remember the melody. She plays, swaying forward and back, forward and back.

"Rosie!" my grandmother is saying. "Come, eat something, es!"

My aunt won't talk about my grandfather. She won't say his name.

Mamma's face is pale.

"Rose, eat!" says my grandmother again.

Softly, into my aunt's ear I whisper, I ask her to play *The Moonlight Sonata*. Aunt Rose sighs and nods. Slowly she begins to play Beethoven. My eyes sting. Mamma is silent. The beauty of the music fills the apartment.

When my aunt finishes the sonata's first movement, she doesn't turn to me. Her soft smile is absent. There's that mark between her eyebrows, a kind of ripple of skin. "Ruthela," she says quietly. "Learn it. Learn to play Beet-hoven, my Rudy."

My aunt's foot hasn't released the pedal. The last note echoes. Her hand is resting on the piano bench. I lace my fingers between hers and she presses them. Her hand feels warm. My legs and arms are weak, rushing with fear. I rest my head on her shoulder. "I promise," I say, our fingers laced together, her hand is so warm against my own, which feels so cold.

A Smile

One night I dream that I'm walking up Carroll Street. A man in a brown hat and winter overcoat walks toward me. He's tall and has a moustache. Just as we pass one another on the sidewalk he turns. He smiles at me. This smile is just for me. It is my grandfather, his face radiant with happiness. He is walking quickly, walking without his cane. He walks on and I do too. His smile is in me now.

I wake up. The bad feeling that has been there every morning, sitting, a stone in my stomach, is gone. The warmth of my grandfather's smile is there instead.

Sleep

Monday afternoon, changing Hannah's clothes, Mamma's voice is a murmur, talking on the telephone with Aunt Dorothy. I hear her in the background of my attention while I'm braiding Hannah's hair, baretting the ends. "But what did Loolie say?" Mamma is asking.

Something in my mother's tone is pulling at my chest, nagging my stomach. I mix up toothpaste and talcum powder and offer Hannah a spoonful. "Here, Hannah, dear," I'm saying. "Here is your rice cereal. "Mmmm."

Mamma has lowered her voice. I strain to hear her. I put down the spoon and tell Hannah I'll be right back. "If you finish it all you can have some dessert."

I take an empty baby peas can I've saved, to fill with water in the bathroom, to dissolve the green sour balls I've collected. "Why is it that no one likes these..." I say softly, "...but Hannah?" Then I'm embarrassed, glad Rebecca isn't home.

I pass the bathroom and walk down the hall to the kitchen instead. Mamma is sitting, hunched up, at the telephone table. She has her back to me. "Loolie and Ben will go," she's saying. "We'll go up on Wednesday." Then she slips into a river of Yiddish, rising and falling and bubbling. There are two words I understand. The first is a word, "hospital." The second is a name. "Rose."

Monday night Rebecca wants to lie down in my bed with me, the way she used to when I was still in my crib. In the dark we listen to our parents' voices coming from their bedroom next door. Leon puts Georgie to bed. Georgie is crying for my mother.

Neither Rebecca nor I mention that a strange quiet has fallen upon the rooms of our house. We don't say that Aunt Rose is spoken so often of these last few days, in whispers and lowered voices. Rebecca and I have a visit, as if we just suddenly want to giggle and talk. We remember funny words we made up when I was three, Georgie's age, and lose our breath laughing. As if Rebecca isn't almost a grown up, as if she isn't almost engaged to be married, she tells me a story, the way she used to when I couldn't sleep.

She tells me about a boy who goes to the store with a shopping list that he drops in a puddle of water and all the ink washes off, so he can't read it. He struggles to remember what it said. "Kidney beans and chocolate syrup and okra," he tells the clerk. Rebecca imitates the look on the clerk's face. We laugh. Then she imitates the mother's face as a pound of okra tumbles out of the bag, along with the clunking onto the table of the can of kidney beans and the jar of chocolate syrup. "Clunk...clunk!" says Rebecca. I'm giggling while she imitates the mother, doing her best to make dinner since they have no money to buy anything else when we hear something and jump. Three sharp knocks from the window wall. Rebecca grabs me.

"What was that?" I whisper.

"I don't know...!" Rebecca answers. We hug each other. I can hear her heart pounding. Then we pull back and peer at each other in the dark. "There's nothing on the other side of that wall but the—back yard—" whispers Rebecca. Then she starts to cry. Then Pappa is at the door.

"What is it?" he's asking, crossing to the bed.

"Pappa, did you hear it?" I ask.

"What, my darling?" answers our father, taking out his handkerchief, wiping Rebecca's tears.

"Pappa, the knocking. Didn't you hear it?" says Rebecca. She's pointing to the window.

"Knocking?" Pappa repeats, looking around.

Pappa crosses to the window. He pulls back the

curtain, opens the window and looks out at the back yard. Pappa's brow is knitted into a frown. "I don't know..." Pappa murmurs. He closes the window and comes back to the bed. Pappa's quiet.

"Pappa?" says my sister.

"Are you going to sleep together tonight?" he asks. But it isn't really a question. He's already tucking us both in, tight and warm, under my sheet and blanket. He smiles, his face is full of care.

"Good night," he whispers, kissing first Rebecca then me. Rebecca and I fall asleep with our arms around each other.

In the morning I'm awakened by Mamma's sobbing. Outside our room in the hall Rebecca and Leon are huddled together. I get out of bed. In bare feet, my eyes half closed with sleep, I make my way to them. Leon puts his arm around me. Then my sister draws me against her. "It's Aunt Rose," she says softly.

"What?" I ask, pulling back to see her face. "Rebecca, what?" She takes my hand. "Ruthie, Aunt Rose—Aunt Rose," my sister is telling me. Her eyes are red and her face looks white and small and beautiful. And I hear my mother, behind the closed door of my parents' bedroom, and my father's voice, soothing.

Leon is curled up into the door frame of our room.

"Aunt Rose—she's had an operation," says Rebecca. And she says something next that I don't understand.

What is that word, Rebecca? I'm demanding, looking at her. But Leon answers, words that bolt through me like cold lightning. I repeat them in a whisper and know I never will again. A sleep. A coma.

My aunt won't wake up.

The three of us are holding each other. Leon's arm is so tight against my head that I can't hear. Why? Why?

floats around inside it.

And I remember the three knocks on the wall from the back yard. Something inside me says, yes. It makes sense now. Something that can't be understood makes perfect sense, in some other world, some world I didn't know existed.

Then I'm thinking of Aunt Rose, standing in the kitchen under the light, in her fuchsia-pink coat with its long belt, the winter I was five. I'm looking up at her, she's smiling down at me, the light from the kitchen, shining around her head. I'm tying and untying that long belt, tying and untying for the first time, knowing I will soon be able to tie my own shoes. My aunt is saying, "You've learned, Ruthie."

Rain

I go to school and come home, do my homework, go to sleep. Pappa writes his articles, Rebecca rolls her eyes when I play with my doll, Hannah. Leon goes to football practice, but everything has changed. After dinner when Mamma does the dishes she talks to God. Then it's quiet in the kitchen and I know that my mother is crying.

My parents and aunts travel upstate to the hospital. Someone is always there with my aunt. Grandma Anna sleeps at Aunt Dorothy's. She comes to our house and cooks. She crochets, sitting quietly on a chair near the stove, in the light from the kitchen window. When I come near she looks up. "Ruthela," she says softly. Her eyes look far away. Their rims are red, the wrinkles underneath are wet.

The first Saturday passes. Mamma doesn't call me from the door of our house, doesn't interrupt the game of potsi that Donna and I are playing down at the corner, in front of Donna's apartment house. Tossing Donna's skate key, we jump the sidewalk, chalked with squares and numbers, our legs crossed as we turn, until Rebecca shouts, telling me it's time to come in for dinner, her voice finding me in the falling dark.

Then two Saturdays, without piano lessons. On the third someone else comes. Mamma introduces Mrs. Seplowitz to Rebecca and me. Rebecca stumbles through *Für Elise*. When my turn comes she asks what I've been studying, she frowns when I tell her.

The Moonlight Sonata, for a child?" the same question my father had asked Aunt Rose, his voice full of gentle surprise. If a child hears something beautiful, Aunt Rose had answered Pappa, she'll be inspired to learn it. Mozart was composing for piano at three. Three! Pappa had exclaimed. Conducting an orchestra at a year old, my aunt had told us then.

I begin to explain this to Mrs. Seplowitz, whose brown penciled eyebrows arch high over her glasses. "You are not Mozart, Child!" Mrs. Seplowitz answers. She frowns as I stumble through the scales. Wrinkles up her face as she takes out a music book for children and pages through it. "We'll work on this! She says, puckering her lips into a spider web of lines. She places the open book onto the music stand. "Now, Child!" she says. We begin work on a piece called "The Little Steam Boat."

I look at the notes on the page and at the words beneath them: put put put put put put put! Goes the little steam boat! Put put put put put put put! Chugging to and fro!

So I begin. "Middle-C-middle-C-put-put-put! La-la-la-la-la-la!" I sing.

Mrs. Seplowitz's gaze turns from the sheet music to

me. I turn to meet it and see that the whites of her eyes, round as checkers, have tiny red veins and yellow raised spots. "Don't sing, Child! Just play!"

"But when my aunt and I play—"

"I am not your aunt, Child!"

My throat tightens. I swallow and turn back to the music. My hands slump against the keys.

"Not that way, Child!" she tells me. "Lift up your hands!"

"Practice your piano," Mamma tells me every day when I come home from school. I can hear her washing dishes in the kitchen, opening cabinets. I can hear the clank of pots, hear her speaking quietly to Georgie, telling him to speak quietly too so she can listen while I practice.

I gaze at the notes of "The Little Steam Boat." until they don't make sense. I'm thinking of Hannah, my doll, sitting in her high chair in my room, wishing I could get up and wander down the hall. I think of my collection shelf. I want to spill my plastic charms onto my bed and count them—the wagons, the pails and shovels, the tiny boots and hats and animals, the ice cream cones. I want to find the delicate silver colored hammer and saw. I want to hold them in my palm, turn and examine them, sort the reds and blues, yellows and greens, and the whites that glow in the dark. Charms with plastic loops for making necklaces or bracelets, which I never do. I just like knowing they're there in the salt water taffy barrel Aunt Dorothy brought back from Miami Beach when I was seven, and which Mamma gave me when the taffy was eaten and my charm collection grew too big for Pappa's green pipe tobacco can.

Then I realize my mother is standing at the archway between the dining room and the living room, asking why it's quiet. Asking, why are you sitting with your hands in your lap? When are you going to practice? Why did we pay good money for you to just sit there?

I look at my mother. I turn to the book of music for children, the page printed with the notes for the piece Mrs. Seplowitz has assigned me. My mother is at the piano now, looking at it too. "The Little Steam Boat?" she asks. She sighs.

I begin to play. My fingers drag on the keys, spilling out too many notes at once. Mamma goes back to the kitchen. I push my hands so my fingers will stumble along. The sound is loud and ugly and Mamma shouts my name from the kitchen door. "Don't bang those keys!" Mamma is shouting. "That's a concert piano, not a toy—I don't know why your father had to have a Steinway," my mother is saying. But she isn't shouting now. She's really talking to herself.

Then she's looking at me from the door. "It's Friday, Ruthie," she says. "Your teacher will be here tomorrow..." and my mother's voice is tired and sad.

I try to imagine Aunt Rose's voice singing *The Little Steamboat*. "La la la la la la," I'm saying. "La la la la la la..." I listen but I can't hear Aunt Rose. Where is she? I want to shout. But I say "la la la la la la" instead, and my voice is louder and now I slap my hands on the keyboard. The ugly sound fills the room. My eyes are stinging, my throat and chest feel like they're breaking apart.

It's Mrs. Seplowitz's voice I hear—"Don't play that way, Child! Child! Child! Child!" There's a knot in my stomach that I don't want to know is there. It's tight and hard and it knows what's happened.

"Ruthie!" Mamma is calling. "You'll ruin that piano! Why did we buy it when your father doesn't know how long he'll have a job?"

I don't know, I'm thinking. I don't know why. I only

know I hate this dark wooden thing and the empty place on the piano bench where my Aunt Rose sat. I only know that when I try to remember her voice singing I only hear the other voice saying, "Child, Child!" Running out of breath, saying, "please, Child!" I can see Mrs. Seplowitz' eyebrows and smell her pink lipstick but I can't hear my Aunt Rose's laughter.

The piano feels like my desk at school, carved with the names of people I don't know. Like a piece of wood that's hard and ruined. I bang the keyboard cover shut. I lay my head on the ledge that holds the sheet music stand.

Mamma is moving through the dining room, feet hurrying, her house dress rustling. "Are we paying for nothing?" she's saying. "Paying for music lessons when your aunt is so sick? Paying when we can't pay for a doctor for my sister to make her well?"

Now my mouth is on the ebony ledge and my teeth have closed over its corner and I'm biting as hard as I can. Ruthie! Mamma is calling from far away. What's the matter with you? Are you crazy? Ruthie, are you crazy?

"I don't want lessons!" I'm shouting at my mother. I hate this piano. Why can't you find a doctor? Why?"

"Because there's no money!" Mamma is shouting. "Because they don't know what to do!" And I see my mother's face drained of color. She's looking at the piano, touching the mark. "My God, Ruthie. How will we sell it now?" Her finger is moving over the half-circle, over the bite that is recorded in the dark wood, wiping away the wet of my saliva with the hem of her dress.

Mamma, Mamma, I'm sorry, I want to tell her. But my voice comes out hard instead. "When will you tell me, Mamma?" I ask.

"What?" Mamma is asking. But she knows. She knows I'm asking her to tell me about my aunt, instead of speaking about it in Yiddish. But she won't tell me, because I'm only a child, only kinde.

Mamma looks over at me. Her hand moves, reaching. I look away.

Georgie and I are sitting in the car. It's raining. The car is parked on a gravel path. I'm reading to Georgie from *The Frog Jamboree*, Georgie's favorite book. I jumble the words, lose my place.

"No," Georgie keeps saying. "Those aren't the right words, Rooty!"

"Let's just look at the pictures for a little while, Georgie," I tell him. Georgie takes *The Frog Jamboree* book away from me and pretends to be reading it himself, turning the pages, pointing to the pictures, saying the words he knows by heart.

I watch the rain sliding down the car window. A group of people huddles in a circle. If I turn my head I can see them. At the front stands a rabbi, my parents, Rebecca, Leon, Aunt Dorothy, Uncle Ben, Aunt Loolie, Aunt Flossie and Grandma Anna. Mamma and Aunt Dorothy are crying. Pappa stands close to them. Uncle Ben's arms are around my grandmother and around Aunt Loolie. My grandmother's head is bent. She's praying, her lips moving. Swaying, she looks so small. Aunt Irene is there and people I don't know. They are burying my Aunt Rose. Georgie and I stay in the car because Georgie is too little to see the open grave, and the wooden box that holds our aunt. How would he ever understand? How can I?

I close my eyes and lean against the cold window glass. Why? The word floats through my head, floats in the rain drumming on the roof of the car, drifts over the black umbrellas, and the rows of stone monuments carved with names. And I see Aunt Rose's face, the only face lit with the sun, as if the sun were shining somewhere else, somewhere far away from this place.

Why? floats and floats and floats in the rain water falling into my head, filling it up, running down my chin, dropping onto my arms and hands, and onto Georgie's book as he holds it out to me. "I can't read it, Rooty. Rooty, I can't read it—Rooty, I want Mamma!"

I open my eyes and look into Georgie's. His forehead is puckered and his warm brown eyes are afraid. Then Georgie is crying. I pull him close to me. "Georgie, I'm sorry," I'm saying. "I'm sorry, Georgie—Georgie,"

I cry with Georgie. I cry with the raindrops streaming on the car, thousands and thousands of them, thousands washing us until Georgie falls asleep in my arms, his sweet breath coming in little, gulped gasps.

Then I hear it—*Rudy!* And I hear the giggle in my Aunt Rose's voice.

"I remembered!" I cry, startling Georgie awake. "Georgie, I remembered!" I'm telling him. "I remembered the sound of her voice!" and now I start to laugh and I look at Georgie and I hug him.

"Rooty—" says Georgie, his voice wavering. "Rooty, is it good?" And I look at Georgie and I smile, and I feel my smile trembling And I rock Georgie, rocking us both.

BOOK FIVE

Grandma Anna

We empty my grandmother's kitchen cabinets, wrapping dishes, putting the food from the refrigerator into bags to take to Montgomery Street, to Aunt Dorothy's.

All but my aunt's concert piano. Mamma says we'll all live on the street before we sell it. Aunt Flossie will keep it in her living room next to her own piano. Aunt Flossie's is the only house big enough for two pianos. "Just for now," says Aunt Flossie. "Someday Rebecca or Ruthie will take it. Rose would want that."

Aunt Rose's piano sits alone in the Carroll Street living room. Its dark ebony form throws a long shadow over the polished wooden floor. "Rosie," I can hear my grandfather saying. "Play something." And I remember the promise I made to my aunt that I would learn *The Moonlight Sonata*. I open the piano bench. The music is sitting right there, on top of my aunt's sheet music and books, just as she'd left it. I take it out and sit down. I begin to play as if my aunt were sitting next to me. Yes, I want to learn this, so we can keep this thing she taught me inside us.

Grandma Anna moves to Aunt Dorothy's. Her bed has been set up in my cousin Joanne's room. This room is also Aunt Dorothy's dining room, where the folding table is set up on Thanksgiving, Passover, and Rosh Hashanah. On the dresser in this room, next to my cousin's "Fire and Ice" red lipstick, a jelly glass now stands. At night it's filled with water and my grandmother's false teeth. Resting near it are Joanne's eyebrow pencils and my grandmother's gray plastic hair combs. My cousin's Chanel Number Five, my grandmother's hair curlers.

My grandmother's snores now come from the door of this room and travel up the hallway to the room where Aunt

Dorothy and Uncle Harry sleep—or used to. Uncle Harry says he doesn't anymore. Aunt Dorothy says it's too hot to close the door. "He closes it, I open it! Who can sleep then?" she asks us, raising her eyebrows.

But Joanne says she could sleep through a tornado, and next to that, my grandmother's snoring is nothing. Grandma Anna and Joanne stay up late talking about the boys my cousin goes out with.

"Mine, mine, mine," says my grandmother, Joanne tells us. "What beautiful children Eliot and I would have! What beautiful children Barry and I would have! What beautiful children Eddie and I would have!" My cousin tells all this to us. But Joanne would have beautiful children with anyone because, like the rest of the women in our family, Joanne is beautiful.

The Window

For three months after Aunt Rose's death, my grandmother sits by Aunt Dorothy's window crocheting. Uncle Harry asks if she'd like to sit outside in the sun, on a folding chair at the side of the building, where a group of people her age likes to sit. My grandmother shrugs.

Everyone worries. My mother talks to God as she washes dishes.

"She's tough," says Uncle Ben. "Look at all she's lived through..."

Pappa says the same thing. "You'll see, Miriam," he tells Mamma.

Sitting by the window, Grandma Anna reads the *Forward*. She plays Solitaire. She hums in her low, raspy voice, the wood of the kitchen rocker creaking as she rocks.

Then one day, Mrs. Ostrow, who came to America on the boat with my grandmother, comes to see her. "Anna, it's enough!" she tells my grandmother. "Put on your coat. There's a Golden Age meeting at the library!"

After that my grandmother is hardly home. On Saturday nights she goes to the movies. The beach on Sundays. She plays cards during the week and takes a bus to Manhattan for theatre matinees.

Again, everyone worries. "Now we have to wait up for my mother as if she's a teenager?" my mother asks God when she washes dishes.

When my grandmother isn't with her friends she's at Uncle Ben's and Aunt Loolie's making matzoh ball soup. Or at our house making kreplach and gefilte fish. Or at Aunt Flossie's making noodle pudding. Aunt Dorothy's freezer is full of dough for rugelach and kichel.

It's true that my grandmother left everything behind her in Russia. And she worked while my grandfather couldn't make a living writing for the newspaper and organizing unions. But when we're by ourselves, and she talks about him or my Aunt Rose, tears gather in the wrinkles under her blue eyes. And sometimes her words are bitter. "He was good, Ruthie. Very, very good. People sometimes took him for the Czar. Your grandfather worked for justice. The Czar..." she shakes her head. "The Czar was a murderer."

Joanne tells us she calls my aunt's name in her sleep.

But she tells me the other stories, too, when we play cards.

On the boat to America, my grandmother was pregnant with Aunt Dorothy. Aunt Ida, my grandmother's sister, got off the boat in France to get her some fresh fruit. The boat was stopping there for an hour. But my aunt got lost, running through the streets, apples and oranges under her arm, wrapped in newspaper, only speaking Yiddish, everyone around her speaking French. The boat began to churn water. My grandmother was frantic. But suddenly there she was. My Aunt Ida had found her way. "I lost my teeth anyway," she tells me laughing. "But I wasn't laughing then, Mamela!"

I look at her as she laughs, as she sniffs back tears.

Small and old, she's strong. And those are the words that go through me. It's a photograph inside me.

Mr. Raphael

"How did this happen?" says Aunt Loolie. "She's alive again!"

One day my mother calls over to Aunt Dorothy's. "Is Mamma there?" she asks my aunt. "She went to a movie? Again?"

"I should be surprised!" my mother says to me. "What?" she asks into the telephone, "With who?" My mother's eyebrows are high. She sits slowly down on the telephone table. Now she's just listening to my aunt. "The third time?" my mother is saying. "He's nice? A widower—ten years!" Mamma's eyes are wide.

Then she listens. "He likes her? Who wouldn't like her? Is he honorable?" When my aunt and Mamma hang up my mother just sits on the telephone table. I look at her, waiting. "Your grandmother is out with—a—Mr. Raphael!" she tells me.

"Mr. Raphael?" I repeat. My mother nods. "What's a widower?" I ask.

"A widower is like a widow. Like—like your grandmother is now. A *widower*—," she repeats, but to herself.

"He must be nice or Grandma wouldn't go to the movies with him," I say.

"He's from The Golden Age Club," says Mamma. "He's the Recording Secretary! He must be responsible—and ten years is a long time." But Mamma isn't talking to me. Her eyes have turned inward.

"He's been Recording Secretary for ten years?" I ask, pulling at Mamma.

"It's ten years since his wife died," says my mother, glancing at me. "At least he isn't rushing into anything—" looking at her hands, turning them over in her lap, looking at the palms, fingering her marriage band. "It's only a year—" says Mamma, her voice trailing off.

I don't point out to my mother that when my grandmother walks down the street you can hear her heels hitting the pavement from around the corner. That all of us, including my brother, Leon, have to hurry to keep up with her. In one day she cooks, sews, cleans, plays cards, then watches her television shows after supper—if she isn't at The Golden Age Club.

When my grandfather couldn't make a living organizing unions and writing for the newspaper, Grandma Anna rented a newspaper stand. She did so well she rented the candy store next door.

"Aunt Dorothy thinks it's good for her," says my mother and sighs. "My God!"

Leon's door opens. "What?" asks my brother. "Aunt Dorothy thinks what's good for who?"

My mother looks at my brother. "Your grandmother has gone to the movies with—a Mr. Raphael—three times!" Mamma tells Leon.

"Oh, yeah!" says my brother. "She told me."

Now Mamma turns to my brother. "My mother is keeping company with a man and she told you?" says Mamma, eyebrows high.

"Maybe they're just friends," says Leon, shrugging.

I'm thinking of my grandfather. My stomach knots. Then I'm thinking, I'm glad we all have to hurry to keep up with my grandmother again. Glad she isn't sitting in front of the window, her cheeks wet with tears. I'm thinking, wouldn't he understand that? Yes, I'm thinking. Yes.

Then Mamma and I are looking at each other. He knew her, Mamma, I want to say. He knew her very well. But I hold the words inside.

"My God!" says Mamma again, putting her hand over her mouth. And I see that she's smiling behind it.

Pappa's Job

The smell of coffee comes from the kitchen. I can hear my parents' voices. Some of their words are just murmurs. Pappa is saying something about our piano teacher, Mrs. Seplowitz. Mamma's answer is an argument.

"We'll find someone else," says my father, loud enough so that his words are clear though they have to travel the length of the hall to my room. "Someone who likes children," says Pappa. Then there are just the sounds of the china coffee cups, the clink of spoons. Mamma says something about the bite mark in the ebony wood of the piano, beneath the music stand. I hear the word, "scar."

"It's not to be sold," I hear Pappa answer.

"When it rains it pours," Mrs. Berman from next door says to my mother. She's snapping her tongue, shaking her head. Her face is full of sympathy.

Pappa is saying it will be a new life.

"What will?" I'm asking.

"We'll work together," answers my father smiling. "As

172

a family!"

My sister, Rebecca, is looking at Mamma, her hazel eyes round, worried. Leon is silent.

"There isn't enough money at the newspaper to support a science column," says my father. We're all silent except Georgie, who doesn't understand why we're sitting on the couch and arm chairs like we're company. "What's a job?" Georgie keeps asking my mother, whose face is a mask of worry. She picks Georgie up and holds him. Georgie puts his fingers in his mouth and pulls on his hair.

"It will be a new life," Pappa repeats.

Looking at us, trying to smile, his eyes are sad. He's telling us we're leaving Crown Street.

At first I can't imagine it. Then the house slowly comes apart. Mamma and Rebecca are packing clothes. The old red couch is put out onto the street for the garbage truck. "We won't need a couch," Mamma says. "There won't be room with the piano. We'll keep the chairs. And when the restaurant is closed we can sit there."

The apartment over the restaurant on Ocean Avenue is smaller than the house on Crown Street. The restaurant Pappa and Mamma have bought with money from the bank. A loan. "We'll have to work hard," my father tells us.

"What will we call it?" he asks. "A restaurant has to have a name!"

"Pincus Luncheonette," says Leon.

"And Candy Store," says Mamma. This makes Pappa smile.

My parents will cook. Rebecca will wait tables. Leon and I will help when we're home from school. Georgie will help with the dishes. Aunt Rose's piano will fit in the restaurant. It will be our turn to have two pianos.

Leon will take the train to school. He has one year left

and the football team. But not me.

"You'll make new friends," Ruthie," my father tells me.

"But what about Donna?" I ask.

"There's the train," answers Pappa. "The restaurant is on the train plaza."

Teams

Saturday morning Donna is talking to Evy Mailman in front of Stevie Berman's house. She turns and sees me. Why didn't you tell me, she's asking. Her black pupils look big in her blue eyes through her glasses.

Evy frowns. Stevie doesn't greet me. How do they know? Then I realize, Rebecca and Leon have told their friends, Aylene's brother. Her cousins. My older brother and sister have known we're moving, only I haven't.

I want to tell Donna that my parents think I'm just a child, too young to tell anything to. But if I speak—if I say, "it's true, I'm moving"—I'll cry.

I'm looking at Donna, almost not recognizing her face because she looks so strange, like someone maybe related to Donna, to my best friend, Donna. Like maybe her cousin or her sister who someone else adopted. The nose and mouth are right, but the eyes look blank, like they don't know me.

I want to tell her that we're opening a restaurant, that we're all going to have to work. But maybe she knows that too. I feel as if I'm moving through water that's full of sand, murky with it, and thick, like at the beach, after a wave pulls up the bottom. My eyes are open but I want to close them against the sharp, salty grit.

Then I see Aylene. She steps out from the shadow. She looks sour. Donna looks over her shoulder toward Aylene.

Then she looks down at the concrete square we're both standing on.

"Punchball," says Aylene. "We're picking teams." Then she looks at me. Donna turns away. Aylene is walking toward Stevie's stoop. Donna is following. Evy, Aylene and my best friend are climbing the first two steps. Dreaming I follow. I stand on the first step, looking up at Aylene, Donna and Evy, who are looking down at me from the second step. Stevie joins them. Gerald Spitzer, Marty Bush and Georgie Goldstein. Carol Parsons crosses the street. Everyone's coming out to play.

"We're choosing teams," Aylene keeps saying. "Mine or Ruthie's," until everyone is standing with Aylene on the second step, looking down at me.

Monnie Greenwald crosses the street. "How come you're moving?" he asks. And the thing is, I can't bring myself to say "my father lost his job." I can't bring myself to say anything because the grit in my eyes will start stinging and I won't be able to do anything but cry.

The faces looking down at me from the second step look strange and angry. If I did cry not even Donna would twist up her mouth. Not even Donna would put her arm around me and lead me away someplace safe where I could just let the hot tears spill down my cheeks. Because Donna isn't even looking at me now. She's just looking down at the edge of the step she's standing on. But Carol Parsons is looking at me. And Carol looks sad. Then she's pulling at Donna's sleeve to come down, and Donna is moving like a rag doll.

I turn and step onto the pavement and walk back to the house, which isn't home.

Alone

The next two weeks pass slowly by. I walk to school alone. The only good thing is that Aylene doesn't look at me anymore. But neither does anyone else. Just the adults and shopkeepers, whose faces seem sad. Everyone knows we're leaving Crown Street.

The rooms of our house are strewn with cartons and newspapers. The rugs are rolled up. Sounds are too loud, echoing off the walls no longer hung with our pictures. Everything is packed, just a few dishes and pots left in the cabinets. A few things folded in my drawers to wear, until moving day.

Mamma, Rebecca and I wash the walls and kitchen cabinets. Leon washes the windows. Pappa washes the floors. Everything looks new, as if we don't live there. We ride in Pappa's Dodge to Ocean Avenue, to the restaurant on the Plaza. Again we clean—the restaurant, and the apartment upstairs. We wash the stoves, the sinks, the glass shelves where food will go, the big refrigerator. Pappa waxes the black and white linoleum-tiled restaurant floor until it reflects the sun, shining through the big front window.

I go out into the courtyard between our building, the one next door and the back of the building that looks out onto the next street. I bounce my pink, rubber Spalding against the brick walls. It isn't a stoop but the sound is sharp and good.

I walk through the rooms upstairs, then wander around the restaurant, trying out the booths with their deep, red, oilcloth-covered cushions that we've scrubbed clean. I run my hands over the lacquered wood tables, stand behind the counter, touch the brass cash register, imagine waiting on customers who have come for lunch or to buy a newspaper.

My mother says we've come full circle. Full circle from Grandma Anna's newspaper stand and candy store to the Pincus Luncheonette. We'll sell the paper Pappa wrote for, and *The Jewish Daily Forward*, where my grandfather wrote about the labor unions.

The moving van comes early on Saturday. Three men, and Pappa, Leon and Sam begin to load our furniture—dressers with their drawers taken out, chairs, the dinette table and cartons with our clothes and books, linens, dishes and pots.

There's nothing for me to do now but walk through the rooms at Crown Street, holding my doll Hannah, to say good bye, listening to my feet striking against the wood floor, down the long hallway to the bathroom. The bathroom mirror is the only mirror left in the house.

"Good bye," I say, looking at my image.

In the living room the baby grand waits for the piano mover. In the silent house, echoing with my footsteps, I walk to the piano bench. I pull open the wooden cover and take out *The Moonlight Sonata*. I sit down and rest Hannah next to me, the place where my aunt used to sit.

"I promised," I whisper, and the sound is loud in the empty room. I begin my practice, looking at the blurred printed notes.

Shadowline

Linda Luxemburg is on her porch playing dolls. One house down, Aylene, Donna, Evy, Joannie Nevins, Freddie Terman and Stevie Berman are playing stoop ball in front of Stevie's house. No one looks over as Sam and Pappa and Leon and Rebecca and me carry furniture and boxes out of the house and load them onto the moving truck. No one looks up as we pack our last things into the cars.

I once had a dream that I stood in the paved space between the Luxemburg's house and ours, looking up at the kitchen window, calling to my mother. She stood at the stove. I wanted to get her attention. But when she turned, it was not Mamma, but a stranger. I woke up, my heart pounding. It was a nightmare.

It will be like that now, I think. Strangers will live here. They'll look up at the light fixture. They'll put their food in the refrigerator. They'll wash their dishes at the sink. In the bathroom they'll use the big, porcelain tub. They'll look out the back window at the Rose of Sharon bush, growing over the fence from Gerald Spitzer's back yard. They'll see the iris bed.

Mamma looks at me as I climb the porch steps one last time. Pappa smiles a sad smile. Mamma reaches for me. I put my head on her shoulder, feel her hot cheek against mine, and salt tears.

We're leaving, even though my grandfather sat on this porch with all of us here. Even though I was born at the hospital down the street.

We make a line, the moving truck, Sam's car, then Pappa's, all driving down Crown Street. Like a funeral procession, we pass from the sunlight of the end where we live to the shadow line, where the maple trees begin, past Stevie's.

I look out the back window. Donna looks up. Her hand shoots into the air and we're waving, waving as we turn the corner, and as we ride down Eastern Parkway, following the truck. I see her as we move slowly into traffic, stopping at red lights. My grandfather smiles from the porch of our house. Aunt Rose is there. She's talking Yiddish with the grown-ups sitting on the green, metal porch chairs. She turns to me. And still my hand is reaching.

And I know that what my father said is true. We're beginning a new life.

Two Pianos

A truck pulls up, Piano Movers in dark blue letters painted along its sides. Three men unload two pianos—Aunt Rose's concert Steinway, and our Baby Grand. Aunt Rose's piano will go into the restaurant. Our piano will be hoisted through the window of the apartment. Two of the men go upstairs. We watch as they remove a frame from the living room window. Then the Baby Grand is making its way up to the second floor on cables, the men calling to each other. I watch as it passes from the daylight into the dark of the apartment.

Mamma sits down in an upholstered living room chair. She mops her face with a kitchen towel. Pappa looks at the driver and the two other men. Pappa smiles. Sit down a moment, he tells them, offering chairs, waiting on the street to start life in our new apartment.

Aunt Rose's piano is standing on the street, under the Brooklyn sky, the sun beating down, warming its ebony wood. The bench is still in the other truck, boxes piled on top. Leon and the movers are still unloading.

I pull a kitchen chair up to the piano, sit down, lift the wooden keyboard cover. I begin—the first notes of the first movement—Beethoven's *Moonlight Sonata*.

Mamma raises the dish towel to her nose. Pappa has turned toward me. So have the piano movers.

Beethoven's notes cover the sounds of car tires floating over cobblestones. A few people have gathered on the sidewalk. Someone crosses the street to join them. They've stopped to listen to my playing, shadows through the music.

I'm making mistakes, pushing the notes out of me. I have to practice, I'm thinking. But the melody is there. The notes are coming from my chest, down my arms, out of my fingers. Inside I'm singing, here it is! Here it is, here it is.

The notes are beautiful in the open air. Is it you playing, Aunt Rose? I'm thinking. But she's in the sun, she's shining in Pappa's eyes. She's in my insides bursting with the melody. And I know it's me who's playing Beethoven, playing to keep my promise to my Aunt Rose. And the notes are like air, and we can breathe again.

Pappa pays the piano movers.

"A piano in the restaurant!" says my mother. "Maybe a customer would like to play. Or an entertainer. Or Rebecca. Or Ruthie."

Pincus's

My new fifth grade teacher, Mr. O'Mara, has blue eyes and he smiles a lot. One day, walking home from school, Peter Granite catches up to me. He's in my class. We talk about school. He asks me what it's like to have moved to Flatbush, the name of this section of Brooklyn, from Crown Heights, where Crown Street is. I tell him about Donna, about stoop ball. About the Solloway's dog, Captain. About rock hunting in the alley. There are no alleys in Flatbush. We agree that we both like Science. Then we just walk, without speaking, until he says, "You play the piano beautifully."

I stop. He stops too. "How do you know?" I ask.

"I heard you play," he answers. "*The Moonlight Sonata*, Beethoven," says Peter. "The first movement."

180

Now I remember, the boy crossing Ocean Avenue, his dark hair falling into his eyes as he walked, the day we moved in. "That was you!" I say, and I smile too.

Two weeks pass and it's as if a tide waited until Pappa opened the restaurant door. Breakfast, lunch and supper—we're busy. Grandma Anna comes and we bake rugelach and pies and apple cake to sell for dessert. Pappa and Mamma cook, and Sam helps on the weekends. Rebecca waits on customers. She seems to have been born to balance a big tray loaded with plates.

Sometimes Peter comes to the restaurant and helps Georgie with the dishes. Sometimes we do our homework in one of the booths, or at an empty table.

Georgie has taken to shouting, "Over easy!" and "Medium rare!" and "Coming right up!" He's seriously learning to wash dishes. The restaurant dishes are too heavy to break.

I sweep the floors and wash the tables. At night, when the "Closed" sign is hung in the window, I practice Beethoven. I practice until my mother calls down to tell me it's time to go to sleep. And I wonder how I could have minded practicing just last year. On Friday nights, Mamma doesn't call. When quiet has settled on the restaurant, I imagine my aunt is listening. When I close the piano and climb the stairs to the apartment everyone is in bed. And sometimes Mamma gets up to tuck me in, a sweater over her nightgown, and tells me my playing is beautiful.

Donna calls and takes the train, and we ride our bikes up and down the streets of Flatbush. We eat lunch in the restaurant. Pappa cooks us hamburgers and Rebecca waits on our table. Donna tells me I'm lucky. She tells me she wishes her family owned a restaurant so that she could eat lunch there. And she tells me about Georgie Goldstein and Marty Bush and Stevie Berman. And Aylene, and Joannie Nevins.

I realize I haven't thought much about Aylene. I haven't looked behind me, walking home from school. I think about how different it is, walking with Peter Granite, instead of wondering whether Aylene's eyes have turned snaky. I shiver, remembering how her face changed. How her eyes looked too green to still be human.

I haven't worried about anyone picking a fight. I sigh with relief as I realize this. Donna looks at me. We smile. She looks down. She looks up again. We twist mouths.

"I don't think she knows what to do with herself anymore," says Donna.

I tell Donna about Peter. I see her eyes through her glasses. I think they're sad. It begins to seem like a long time has passed since we moved.

Pappa and I put Donna and her bike on the train. We wave until her train disappears around the turn. And it seems so strange.

With two pianos the house is filled with music. Rebecca plays upstairs, and I play Aunt Rose's piano, downstairs. Sometimes I play when people are eating and they applaud. I practice *The Moonlight Sonata* until Yom Kippur, the Jewish day of atonement. At night the family gathers to break the fast together. That night I play. Everyone cries, even my Uncle Ben. And I miss Aunt Rose.

Circles In The Sand

Wednesday morning my grandmother telephones. "Ruthela," she says. "Sunday, we're having a beach party with Mrs. Ostrow and the others. How would you like to come, Mamela?" My grandmother and Mrs. Ostrow, who I call Aunt Sophie, came to America on the same boat.

"Sunday?" I look at my mother. She nods at me over a sink of dishes. "No one will be home," she says. "Go."

"But Mamma, I'll be the only child."

My grandmother chuckles at the other end of the telephone. "Sweetheart, you'll be the guest of honor," she says. "You'll have a good time."

My mother is looking at me, waiting for my answer.

"Okay, Grandma," I finally say.

"Don't worry, Mamela," says Grandma Anna. "Kishkas and salami sandwiches, your favorite. See you Sunday!"

I love my grandmother's kishkas. Rebecca turns green when my grandmother brings them. "What are cowww's intessstiiiines?" asks Georgie when Mamma cuts a piece for him to taste. "They're insides. Ya'know, the stuff in here, in their stomachs," Leon tells Georgie matter-of-factly. Georgie's brow furrows. His eyebrows twist. Then he starts to cry. "Shah, Darling," says Mamma. Then she reprimands Leon. "Georgie is sensitive," she tells my brother. What she means is that Georgie cries if someone looks at him.

My grandmother calls Thursday. "I'll pack cucumbers," she says. "Olives, Ruthela," she tells me Friday. "Bring a hat, it will be haase," she says on Saturday.

"Grandma, what is haase?"

"Hot," my mother calls from the stove, where she's preparing roast chicken for forty, the Saturday night restaurant regulars.

"Don't forget your bathing suit, Darling," says my grandmother on Sunday morning. "So we can go into the vasser."

183

"Grandma, what is vasser?"

"Water! Calls my mother from the restaurant stairs.

"Swimming," says my grandmother. "We'll go swimming, Darling."

"You can wear your new bathing suit," Mamma says when I hang up the telephone.

My new bathing suit is blue. Mamma and I bought it on sale in September.

"Mamma, it's too big!" I had said. "Next year it will fit," my mother had answered.

I put it on now and look in the mirror. How did she know? It fits perfectly, ribbed and ruffled. Where the top looked like my grandmother's shower cap last year is now filled in. And there's a curve at my waist where last year it was straight. I rummage in the kitchen drawer for a grocery bag. I fold the bathing suit and slip it inside with a towel.

Pappa drives me to Montgomery Street. My grandmother is waiting downstairs.

"Mamela!" she greets me. "Come, I have to put away the garbage, then we'll go!" She's holding two paper bags. "You brought your bathing suit?" I hold up my bag. We go through the side door of her building, into the basement. "I was about to throw it away upstairs, then Sophie called and I forgot—mine mine mine!" she exclaims, shakes her head, her tongue snapping.

"Here, Darling, give me your bag." She opens one of her paper bags and puts mine inside. "Na, hold this, Ruthie!" she says, giving me the bag when we get to the dumbwaiter.

The dumbwaiter, the little elevator car that travels up and down the six floors of my grandmother's apartment building, brings the garbage to the superintendent, Mr.

184

Hanrahan. My grandmother pokes the bell and opens the door.

"Mr. Handleman!" she cries up the shaft, which smells of sour garlic. Now she plays the bell like a piano note. But the sound is like a fire engine bell. It pierces the Sunday morning quiet of the building. "Mr. Handleman-n-n!" she calls again.

"It's Hanrahan, Grandma," I whisper.

First there's silence. Then the door of the first floor dumbwaiter opens. "It's Sunday, Mrs. Bailenson," answers the Super hoarsely.

"It's the garbage!" Mr. Han-Handleman!" calls my grandmother.

"Hanrahan, Grandma," I remind her.

"Mrs. Bailenson," answers the Super, after a moment. "Sunday is my day off!"

"But the garbage, Mr. Han-Haner-Handleman—it has no day off!" my grandmother calls up the shaft. Another silence, then Mr. Hanrahan sighs. "Close the door, Mrs. Bailenson," he grumbles. My grandmother closes the dumbwaiter door and the cables come to life, groaning, snapping, until the little elevator car stops in the basement. My grandmother opens the door. "Here, Mamela, give this to me," says Grandma Anna, taking the bag and setting it on the wood platform. "Here it comes, thank you very much, Mr. Ha-Ha-Hameir!" she cries before shutting the door. "There!" she says with satisfaction, pressing the button that sends the car into motion.

"Kishkas and salami!" says my grandmother, shaking the other bag as we walk outside into the sunlight.

My grandmother's legs are short. They bulge with muscles. We hurry toward the Avenue. Waves of heat rise from the sidewalk. "I can't wait to swim!" I say.

"We'll eat first," says my grandmother.

"But Grandma, it's hot—haase," I say. Grandma Anna smiles, kisses me.

"We'll swim, then we'll eat. Then we'll rest and swim again—and eat!" Her big dress is flapping. Her cut-out leather shoes are thumping their stubby heels on the pavement as she hurries along. I hurry to keep up.

At the bus stop she hands me the paper bag while she looks for change. My mother bought my grandmother a canvas bag that she won't use. "A paper bag is a modern invention!" she told my mother. This one has a grease stain and smells a little like fish.

At last the bus appears in a cloud of fumes. Its brakes squeal and the door opens. My grandmother hands me our two dimes and I put them into the glass change machine.

The machine jingles as the coins jog through its passages like a pinball machine, until they come to rest on a pile of nickels and dimes sitting on the bottom. We find a seat. "Give me the bag," says my grandmother, taking it and setting it on her lap. She bends her head and sniffs. "I thought I took a fresh one," she says. Her head is tilted, she's puzzling. Past the open window the hot sidewalk and buildings are passing, until the bus is flying, and they're a blur. I feel the hot breeze and think of the cool water of the ocean.

At the train station Aunt Sophie is waiting. Six stops to Riis Park, Aunt Sophie and my grandmother speak in Yiddish. I gaze into the subway tunnel as lights pass outside the window—red, green, yellow, white, some the same blue as my bathing suit.

"Anna!" calls Mr. Raphael around his cigar as

we emerge into daylight upstairs. "Hallo, Ruthie!" Mr. Raphael is wearing a straw hat. He's carrying a canvas beach chair and a white bakery bag. His cigar is clenched in his teeth, unlit. "Dessert!" he calls around it, swinging the bag. Mr. and Mrs. Greenbaum, Mrs. Newman and Mrs. Feigelman, my grandmother's friends from The Golden Age Club, arrive on the next train. We walk two blocks to the beach. Soon my grandmother and her friends are talking and laughing, telling stories, bags and blankets forming a circle on the sand.

"Grandma, let's change into our bathing suits," I say.

"Ruthie, Darling," Let's eat a little first—everyone's hungry."

"But then we'll have to digest!" I complain.

"Anna," says Aunt Sophie. "We'll eat, Ruthie will swim. We'll watch her!"

"Azai gut!" says my grandmother—it's good! "Come, Darling, we'll change in the bath house." My grandmother picks up our paper bag. "Ruthela, look at the waves, mine mine mine, how beautiful!" she says, her tongue popping. She opens the bag. "Wha-at's this?" she says, then slips into Yiddish.

"Oi!" cries Aunt Sophie. Mr. Raphael takes the cigar from his mouth. "What, Grandma?" I'm asking. My grandmother is looking from the bag to me. A feeling starts in my stomach. "Darling—maybe he didn't burn the garbage yet—it's Sunday, his day off—Mr. H-Han... Ruthie...!"

My mouth is trying to move to answer.

My grandmother looks stricken. "Mamela...we sent the bathing suit to Mr. H—to the Super—Darling...It went up the dumbwaiter...we brought the garbage to the beach!" she finishes.

"The kishkas too?" Mrs. Greenbaum is leaning forward in her beach chair.

"Yeh," my grandmother murmurs.

"The bathing suits...?" asks Mr. Raphael, looking from my grandmother to me. "Yeh," says my grandmother. She looks lost. Then she starts to cry, tears zigzagging through her wrinkles.

"An—nna," says Aunt Sophie, her tongue popping like corn. Mr. Raphael hurries over with his handkerchief, trying to give it to both of us. Aunt Sophie brings a paper napkin. My grandmother's arms are around me. I'm blowing my nose into the napkin. She's blowing hers, behind my head, into the handkerchief. "Mamela, Mamela," she's murmuring.

Blue, blue, blue, blue—the words are drifting through my mind along with the ruffled skirt, the elastic top of my bathing suit hugging my waist. "Grandma, it's okay," I'm sobbing, but blue blue blue blue rides on the waves, blurred and slapping against my head and out though my eyes. I'm sucking in my breath, squeezing my nose into the napkin, and I can't stop crying.

"Sweetheart, we'll buy a new bathing suit. I'm so sorry, Ruthie, Darling." My grandmother is wiping my tears with the handkerchief. "Come to the water, let's wash your face, Sweetheart."

"Anna, Ruthie, have a Bialastocker Roll," says Aunt Sophie. But I'm not hungry.

My grandmother accepts the roll. She blows her nose again. We walk down to the water and I wash my face. My grandmother is tearing pieces off the roll, small enough for her to chew with her false teeth. She's facing the ocean. The sun is shooting shafts of gold off the waves. "All that good food up in smoke!" my grandmother says, dabbing at her eyes. Then she stops chewing. "Did I say smoke? Smoke? Smoke smoke sm—oww—ke? Ruthie, Darling, where's that garbage?"

"The garbage?" I repeat.

"Yeh—mamela, we'll make a nice fire, we'll make a feast, tell stories! Come, it will be fun." My grandmother is saying this, hurrying back up the beach to the blanket, me hurrying after her. Now she's dumping garbage onto the sand, "Everything happens for the best! Look, you'll see, there's plenty that's good here!" Wrinkled paper and torn boxes, fish skin, orange rinds, onion peels and a soup bone tumble out of the bag onto the blanket. "Gut, gut, azai gut!" my grandmother is murmuring. "Garbage for the seagulls, garbage for us! Harry! Put this over there—they'll love this herring!"

Grandma Anna is clapping her hands, "Cum! Cum!" she's crying. A crowd of gulls relocates, some walking quickly on their long, spindly legs, others flying, from the other end of the beach. Crying out they begin diving for the fish skin. "Look at how they love it!" my grandmother is saying, popping her tongue. "Let's see—here, Darling, rinse these out! We'll fill them with some nice shells to show your mamma!" She hands me three glass jars. They're greasy, stuck with chicken feathers.

At the water's edge I rub the jars with salt water and sand. Feathers float on the waves. My grandmother and her friends are sorting through my grandmother's garbage, laughing, speaking to each other in Yiddish. "We need more paper!" my grandmother calls. So now I'm gathering other people's garbage, ice cream wrappers, paper bags, newspaper. Grandma Anna stuffs it all into her own bag of garbage. She glances at the lifeguards, who are looking in our direction. Maybe they think we're cleaning the beach. Then my grandmother chuckles. "We'll wait until they leave. They're young boys, they don't want to spend the evening on the beach with a bunch of old people! Come, Sweetheart, we'll swim in our clothes."

We swim and eat rolls and cheese and babka—sugared pound cake with raisins.

We drink lemonade and swim again. The sun dries my shorts and polo shirt. I listen to the murmur of waves and voices and doze until I think my mother is calling me for school. But it's Grandma Anna. "Ruthie, wake up! It's five o'clock." That's too early, I think, and sit up. "Look!" says my grandmother, nodding to the lifeguards climbing the boardwalk stairs. "I thought they'd never go home!" Now we're the only ones left on the beach. "Nice and quiet," says my grandmother. Her eyes are on the bath house. The lifeguards come out, dressed in long pants, and cross the street. My grandmother watches them until they're out of sight. "Harry!" she calls. "Na! Where's your lighter?"

"We'll need some wood," says Mr. Raphael. Then, Aunt Sophie, the Greenbaums, Mrs. Feigelman—all of us, are scavenging the beach for driftwood. With her hands, my grandmother hollows out a hole in the sand. We make a pile of the bags and wrappers and newspapers, an egg box from my grandmother's garbage, the box from the candles she and my aunt burned for my grandfather's Yartzeit—the anniversary of his death. My grandmother arranges the wood on top. "Here goes!" she calls. She spins the wheel of the cigar lighter and the pile catches.

All around the circle tongues are popping. The fire is crackling, throwing sparks. Mr. Raphael is chuckling. "Mine mine mine," my grandmother murmurs. "Na, Ruthie, here." She opens her purse. "A dollar—get a pound of hot dogs from the kosher butcher, hurry before he closes. Three stores up from the corner—go!"

While the hot dogs roast on sticks I fill the jars with pebbles for my rock collection, shells and smoothed sea glass. I think of Crown Street, Georgie Goldstein, Davine Hoffman, Stevie Berman, Marty Bush, Monnie, Carol Parsons, Donna and Aylene. Maybe they're riding their bikes on this Sunday afternoon, and playing stoopball. Maybe the people who have moved into our house on Crown Street have children. Maybe they're all playing stick ball, or potsi, or Ringelivio.

With a jar top I make circles in the sand, and watch the waves erase them. Then we eat, my grandmother and her friends telling stories about the lives and families they left in Poland and Lithuania.

"We were young, like you, Ruthie," Mrs. Feigelman is saying.

"Where did you learn to build a fire, Grandma?" I ask.

"In Poland, in my mother's stove!" my grandmother answers. Then she's humming in her low, scratchy voice, her arm around my shoulders, rocking us both. Stars look like diamonds on the sea. The sky is crowded with them, and a trail of smoke from the dying embers of my grandmother's fire. From across the circle, Mrs. Newman smiles at me. The sound of a car horn drifts over the sand from the street.

On the way home I nod against Grandma Anna, rocked by the clattering subway train. Lights streak past the window in the dark tunnel: white, yellow, green, red, bathing suit blue.

"Ruthela!" says my grandmother through the telephone the next day. "Darling, you'll never guess! Mr. Han—Mr. Han—the Super—rang the bell this morning. He found your bathing suit! He thought it was a bag of rags—just some old schmates, imagine! Then he smelled

191

the salami and kishkas. They didn't smell too good. He said your bathing suit looked too new to be garbage. So I gave him kishkas—fresh! It's here, Mamela—your bathing suit!"

"Grandma! Grandma!" I'm saying, listening to my grandmother's laughter through the telephone, and I'm laughing too. "It was good, Grandma," I'm saying. "It was fun!"

"Listen, Ruthie..." she says after a minute. "You'll come again, maybe sometime? Sunday—it will be—hot! This time we'll get a good tan," she says. "The others will be there, we'll have a nice fire, Bubela."

"Sunday?" I ask. If I were at Crown Street, I'd be playing on the street with my friends. "I—have nothing else to do..." I tell my grandmother. And I know she's heard it, the ache in my throat.

"Nothing else to—" the telephone goes quiet. "Listen, Ruthie...you'll be the star, the guest of honor! Everyone will be so glad to see you, Darling, come!"

My eyes are stinging. Then my grandmother and I are talking at the same time. "Yes! Yes!" I'm saying.

"Yeh! Yeh! Yeh!" she's saying. "Ye—yes!"

Ruthela, we have a new story to tell. A story is better than food! We'll tell about Mr. Handleman, Mr. Han—ra—Mr. Hanra—man—about the Super—the bathing suit, my darling. Mine, mine, mine! You'll look so beautiful wearing it, I'll be so proud!" she's saying, her tongue snapping and popping.

Midnight Green

Late at night, in the kitchen at the back of the restaurant, my parents are drinking coffee. The album of family pictures is open on the long rectangular table, where the family eats dinner, and where, by day, my parents prepare food. The album's pages are made of black paper. Black ridged, paper corners, with glue backs, hold snapshots of my grandmother, my grandfather, Pappa's friends posing with hats and cigars, making faces. And Mamma, her sisters and her cousins, wearing suits and hats and bathing suits. In these pictures Mamma is looking full-faced at the camera.

I am at the sink making Hannah some dinner, struggling to cream the shampoo and talcum powder Aunt Dorothy brought me from her vacation in Miami Beach. "The Miami Hilton" is printed on the bottle of shampoo and on the tiny, cylindrical powder box. I'm adding water in drips from the faucet, pressing out the lumps with a fork.

When it looks enough like oatmeal I start back to my room. But I catch sight of a picture and stop: Mamma in her white satin wedding gown. At her tiny waist is a sash with a jeweled buckle.

"My moustache was dark," says Pappa.

"Mamma's veil," murmurs my mother, touching the picture softly. "It will be beautiful around Rebecca's blond hair. Where is the veil?" says Mamma suddenly, looking up.

"How can it be, Miriam?" says Pappa, absorbed. "It was only yesterday that my brother held it behind you!"

Mamma looks distracted. "I don't remember packing it..." she's saying. "My God...I wonder if Loolie has it!"

Pappa turns to me. "Your mother is beautiful," he tells me. Mamma turns to my father and makes a face. Then she looks at me. She smiles and her cheeks flush.

I just can't picture my sister, Rebecca, getting married.

"What's wrong with her?" asks Leon. All she talks about is Sam! Then he mimics my sister. "Sam's the smartest person I know."

"He's so-o-o strong!" follows Georgie. Then he puts two fingers into his mouth.

"She's buying dishes!" exclaims Leon, his voice high-pitched and cracking.

Georgie pulls his fingers from his mouth and snorts with laughter. "We don't need any more dishes!" he says. Then he looks confused.

Leon stands there nodding. "I mean look at the kitchen—how many more dishes do we have room for?"

I look at my two brothers and shake my head. "Don't you think she might want her own dishes?" I ask.

Leon looks at me. Suddenly his eyes clear. "Sam," he says.

"They're getting married," I say.

"Sam," says Leon again.

"Sam," I repeat.

"Sam?" asks Georgie.

"He'll be our brother in law!" declares Leon.

I nod.

"What's a brother in law?" asks Georgie.

Leon looks down at Georgie. "In the eyes of the law Sam will be our brother," answers Leon. Then he turns back to me, his eyebrows going one way, his mouth another.

"What is the law?" asks Georgie.

"The law?" repeats Leon, turning back to Georgie. "The law? The law-is—the rules-of—a—country. Our country. By the rules of our country, the—uh—United States of—America, Sam will be our brother—by law."

For a moment Georgie is silent, looking up at Leon. "But why?" he asks softly.

194

"Because he's marrying our sister," Leon answers. "When did this happen?" he says looking at me.

"What is marrying?" asks Georgie, pulling on Leon's shirt.

I shift my weight to the other foot. This may take some time.

"Sam and Rebecca," Leon is saying to Georgie, "they'll be married—like Mamma and Pappa! How come no one told me?"

Well where were you, Leon, I want to say. In some other household? On some other planet? But I just roll my eyes.

Georgie puts his two fingers back into his mouth. He stares at the wall and sucks on them. Now Leon is staring at the wall too. I'm staring at Leon and Georgie. My face feels strange. My stomach feels fluttery.

"How will we do everything?" Rebecca moans at supper.

"We will do everything, Rebecca, Darling," says Mamma. Her voice is hard with resolution.

Rebecca's head is on the table. My mother sits down and puts an arm around her. But she sighs. She's worried. "Everything!" she repeats, and kisses my sister's blond hair.

"Oh, Mamma," says Rebecca, lifting her head, looking into my mother's eyes. Mamma smiles and touches Rebecca's cheek. How can she sound that crazy way? I'm wondering. Her eyes look round and daffy, as if she's been hypnotized.

After dinner Pappa lingers over his coffee. "Didn't we just dance at our own wedding, Miriam?"

My mother is at the sink. She turns, puts down her dish towel, looks at my father and sighs. Then she looks at the four of us, Rebecca, Georgie, Leon and me and nods.

She covers her mouth, closes her eyes, shakes her head. She looks at my father and they both begin to laugh. Then Rebecca laughs, sounding daffy. Georgie's looking at Rebecca. Leon's looking at me. I'm shrugging, pressing my lips together.

My brothers get new suits. The tailor makes Pappa a new shirt.

"Mamma, can I try on the veil?" asks Rebecca.

"I have to find it," answers Mamma. "It has to be washed.

"My God!" exclaims my sister. "What's Ruthie going to wear? She'll need a dress!" She says this as if I'm not there.

"Of course she will," answers my mother, without correcting my sister for saying, 'My God.'

"We'll go to Malka's," says Mamma.

"Malka's!" my sister whispers.

I'm thinking... *Are you getting married? Come to Malka's! The most exclusive bridal shop in Brooklyn, New York, serving all five boroughs and the world.*" The advertisement for Malka's is on the dining room table along with a clutter of invitations and lists.

"A flower girl dress," says Rebecca, turning to me. She smiles, looking that daffy way. "Something in organza!" she says.

What is organza and why is this strange person looking at me this way? I wonder vaguely, returning her smile.

Mamma looks for Grandma Anna's veil. She looks in the attic. She looks in Grandpa's steamer trunk in the basement. "It will turn up!" she says, cheerily. "No-*thing* to worry about!" she tells us.

The guest list is three pages. We address envelopes to

196

Pappa's cousins, Gertie and Sol, and their twins, in Philadelphia. To Mamma's cousin, Mordecai, whom we've never met, in Ohio.

Passing my parents' room, I see my mother kneeling. She's emptying the cedar chest, pulling things and tossing them onto the floor. "Where have I put it?" she says, standing up. Then she sees me. She looks startled. Her face falls. "It's got to be somewhere!" she confides. Now Rebecca is behind me, leaning into the room. "Does Grandma have it?" she asks.

Mamma flushes. She calls Grandma Anna. "Mamma?" says our mother. "We're looking for the lace veil for Rebecca. Yes? You gave it to me when you moved from Carroll Street? Are you sure? Yes. Yes. No. No. Don't worry, I'll find it. It's got to be here. Of course I will, Mamma!" Then she slips into Yiddish.

"The queen of France had one just like it!" she declares after she hangs up the telephone.

"The queen of France?" repeats Georgie. Mamma nods. Her shoulders sag.

At the table Pappa and Mamma are talking quietly, about money. "We've got everything," says Mamma. "A back yard full of flowers and a restaurant full of space. Dan will take the pictures. Rebecca has written the invitations, Flossie will play the piano, everyone will bring something for the table. And the rabbi won't mind waiting. What else is there?" My parents are looking at each other. "The tailor," says Pappa. "Malka," says Mamma.

Mamma folds her hands. "God will provide," says Pappa, softly.

Sam comes over. Mamma searches through the closets. She pulls out boxes that are still not unpacked. "That veil is one of a kind!" says Mamma.

"I thought the queen of France had one," says Georgie.

Mamma frowns. "Two of a kind," she tells my brother, Georgie.

"It's a bad omen," my sister moans.

"Don't say such a thing!" says my mother. She hugs my sister with one hand, waving the other in Sam's direction, cleaning the air of omens. "Sookie wore it last, I'll call her." My cousin Sookie is Aunt Loolie's and Uncle Ben's daughter.

"Sookie, Darling?" says Mamma into the telephone. "How is the baby? What? Going to camp this summer? A baby going to camp? Imagine! Where does the time go? He's going to be eight!" Mamma covers the receiver. "My God, soon there will be a Bar Mitzvah!"

"Sookie, Grandma Anna's veil, where is it, Sweetheart? No, we haven't found it yet. The wedding will be here before we know it. No? No." Mamma is shaking her head, frowning at the floor. "Of course—it's got to be somewhere. Thanks, Darling, send my love."

Rebecca's chin is resting in her hand. Her face is turned to the wall. Sam looks gloomy. His stiff, white collar is too large for his skinny neck. I don't know why my sister likes him so much. Enough to marry him? I'm asking myself.

Mamma is preparing linens, washing them, rolling them up, storing them in the refrigerator. As the days pass I iron napkins, smelling the starchy steam, folding them, pressing sharp creases. Mamma does the tablecloths. She tucks lavender sachet between the folds. We look at them with satisfaction. They sit, waiting, in piles on Mamma's dresser. "Someday you'll get married, Ruthie," says Mamma.

"If I do," I tell her, "I'll marry someone like Pappa."

My mother smiles. "Sam will be good for Rebecca," she

says softly. "He's practical. He'll be a good provider."

"Pappa's a good provider," I say.

Mamma is silent.

I turn to see her face. Her head is lifted, her eyes are looking at the ceiling. "Pappa is a scientist. A writer. He works very hard. We all work hard." Mamma sighs, then laughs. "Sam will go out and earn a living." She says. "Good for Rebecca, good for the family."

The family, I'm thinking. Our family. Sam will be part of our family.

Sam's parents come. Mamma introduces them to us, "Mr. and Mrs. Prezant." Sam's father is skinny like Sam. Sam's mother isn't. She wears perfume. She looks around at the restaurant, talking with Mamma and Pappa and Mr. Prezant. Her eyes examine the big stove, the tall refrigerator. The smell of "April in Paris" lingers in the restaurant after Sam's parents leave.

My parents sit at the table looking at the photo album. "Rebecca Prezant," says Mamma.

"Who will believe we have a married daughter?" says Pappa.

Mamma laughs. She leans her shoulder into my father's.

In their wedding picture Pappa's hair is thick. He's turned toward Mamma. Mamma is looking into the camera, glowing. The lace veil frames her face. "Dan took these," murmurs Pappa.

"Where could it be?!" says Mamma, remembering the veil. She dials Aunt Loolie. "Am I calling too late?"

Aunt Loolie doesn't have the veil.

"I can't understand it!" Mamma tells Aunt Loolie. "I know she brought it from Russia! Who doesn't know? It isn't lost, we'll find it!" Mamma hangs up the telephone and drops into a chair. She covers her face with her hands.

"Loolie will call Rachel. It can't be nowhere." My cousin Rachel is Aunt Loolie's and Uncle Ben's other daughter.

Leon is upset. His team is playing a football game the day of the wedding. "Who'll play quarterback?" says Leon.

"Someone else," says Rebecca.

"Who?" asks Leon. I'm the best they've got!"

"Who'll hold up my veil?" says Rebecca.

"What veil?" asks Georgie.

Rebecca starts to cry. "Darling, shah!" says Mamma. She looks angrily at Leon. "We'll find it, you'll see," she tells my sister. "There's still time."

Aunt Flossie sews a ring cushion for Georgie to carry. It has a lace ruffle.

"I'll look like a girl!" declares Georgie, looking at my mother in disbelief.

"A girl?" says our mother. "No! You'll look handsome!" Georgie is crying, rubbing his eyes.

"Georgie," says Mamma. "We'll take off the ruffle! What will I tell Flossie?" she says to the florescent light fixture.

Pappa lifts Georgie onto his lap. Georgie buries his head in Pappa's shoulder.

Cousin Rachel calls to say she doesn't have the veil. "Flossie?" says Mamma. "Why would Flossie have it? She washed it? I'll call her." Aunt Flossie is sure she gave it to my mother to pack away for Rebecca. "Flossie, I can't remember!" Aunt Flossie says she'll look for it.

We go to Malka's. Malka wears glasses that are attached to a ribbon around her neck.

They have no handles. Malka wrinkles her nose to keep them from falling off. Malka brings Rebecca gowns. I count seventeen then lose track. My sister doesn't like any of them, looking at herself in the mirror, shaking her head.

"Darling, take off your sneakers," suggests Mamma.

Malka brings Rebecca a pair of satin slippers. Mamma tells Malka about the missing veil. Malka brings another veil.

"Made en Par-ee!" she tells Mamma. Mamma looks at the veil. She turns it over in her hands, holds it to the ceiling light. She frowns. "It's not the same," she says.

Malka shrugs. Rebecca sits down.

"Sweetheart—Rebecca—Grandma's veil will turn up."

The sky grows dark against the window mannequins. I look at Malka's soft carpet, imagining lying down. No one would notice, I'm thinking. Rebecca keeps trying on dresses. Hundreds of them. Thousands. I close my eyes. Maybe just a nap. I'm actually asleep though I'm still standing, and dream I'm in my bed, Hannah lying next to me, because Rebecca's voice suddenly wakes me.

"It's perfect! Mamma!" she's saying. Her face is lit up. "Pure silk," says Malka. "The beads are French glass. Made en Par-ee!"

I feel dizzy.

Now my mother and Rebecca are taking dresses off the rack, holding them against me. I'm too groggy to care. "Ohh, Sweetheart," my mother is saying. "This is just right!" I look down at the dress of blue organza, with its pink chiffon top and satin tie. Rebecca pulls it over my head. Maybe I'm still dreaming, smiling in my sleep, like babies do.

Mamma tries a velvet gown. Its deep green color looks beautiful next to her fair skin. My sister and I look at each other.

"Midnight Green for the mother of the bride!" sings Malka. But it's a soft song. She's looking at Mamma through her glasses, wrinkling her nose.

Mamma is looking in the mirror. "Mamma," murmurs my sister. Mamma turns to us and giggles.

Sam comes every night for dinner. We sit at the long table in the restaurant kitchen. Sam talks with Pappa about electricity and radio waves. He carries pencils in his shirt pocket and a fountain pen that sometimes leaks. He sits straight in his chair, but his eyes move around the table, touching Mamma's, Georgie's, Leon's, mine. His eyes are blue. They twinkle, as if he's just on the edge of laughter. Sam looks different, I'm thinking.

Rebecca leans her chin on her hand, looking sideways at Sam, smiling and sighing. Pappa drinks his soup and looks around at us all too. He looks happy. It dawns on me—Sam is here to stay. My stomach feels like it's full of grasshoppers.

Rebecca and I do the supper dishes. "I guess you really like him," I say quietly. Rebecca looks over her shoulder at Sam, still sitting at the table, talking with my parents. Then she looks at me and laughs. "You will too, Ruthie," she says.

We're both silent. "Next time we go to the beach want to come?" I turn to see her. We're standing there smiling, just looking at each other. I glance at the table and catch Sam's eye. He smiles. I imagine us all at the beach, Sam in a bathing suit. I'm wearing my blue bathing suit. Sam is laughing, splashing in the water. I realize I've never heard Sam actually laugh. *My brother in law* sails through my head. And Leon's words: *the rules of our country!*

Aunt Flossie calls. "No?" says Mamma into the telephone. She's exhausted. She turns away, avoiding my

202

sister's eyes.

"It's gone!" says my sister. "Why is this happening, Mamma?"

"Sweetheart, nothing is happening," my mother is saying softly, stroking my sister's hair. "It has to be somewhere—doesn't it?" she's asking quietly.

My grandmother comes. She and my mother are going shopping for my grandmother's shoes. My grandmother hugs Rebecca. "How beautiful you'll look, Sweetheart," she says. "Mine mine mine," my grandmother is saying, snapping her tongue. There are tears in her eyes. "Now it's your turn to wear the veil. If only they could see you. But they will!" she declares, her face lighting up. "Wherever they are—may they be in Heaven—they will!" All this while she's hugging my sister. Rebecca looks miserable over my grandmother's shoulder. Mamma's mouth is pinched shut.

The days pass and the phone keeps ringing. My aunts are baking kugals. Pappa will roast a turkey. Gifts are piling up in the rooms upstairs. Folding chairs clutter the hall. "A restaurant and we need more chairs?" asks Leon. I'm wondering if there will ever be anything to think about again but Rebecca's wedding. And the veil.

A week before the wedding it hasn't turned up. My mother is washing dishes, looking at the ceiling, talking to God. "It crossed the sea!" she's telling God. "My mother wore it, my grandmother wore it! My sister wore it! And my daughter??" she's asking. Then more questions, in Yiddish, but it's too late. Rebecca comes out of her room. "I'm the only one in the whole family...!" she cries, also to the ceiling.

"Rebecca, come! I need your help with the

dishes—Darling, please!" Mamma's holding out a dish towel. "Please, Rebecca, you'll make yourself sick!" Then Mamma is washing, looking up at the ceiling. Rebecca is drying, looking into the sink.

The evening before the wedding, Sam is at the door. But Mamma won't let him in. Mamma blocks Rebecca from his view, holding up her hands. "The groom can't see the bride before the ceremony!" declares Mamma. Rebecca peers around Mamma at Sam. Sam looks miserable.

Again we wash the windows. Pappa waxes the tables and floors. Mamma calls Malka. She comes with her veil. Long past bedtime we're still laying the tables, dressing them in the starched tablecloths and napkins, setting them with silver.

I lie awake, listening to my sister crying. Georgie comes to our bedroom door. I tell him to go to sleep. "What's so important about a stupid veil?" he asks Rebecca. "At least you have Sam!"

Rebecca looks startled. She looks at Georgie and stops crying. "Oh, Georgie," she whispers.

In the morning Pappa hangs a sign he's written on the restaurant door. "Closed for Rebecca and Sam's Wedding." Leon climbs the ladder to hang white paper streamers from the ceiling. At the back of the restaurant, Pappa moves the pie cabinet to make room for the wedding canopy—Sam's prayer shawl. Pappa and Sam drape the shawl over a frame Pappa has built.

"Like a tent," says our father.

Georgie asks if we can move it into the courtyard after the wedding so he can sleep outside. Pappa picks him up so he can touch it. "It's a symbol," my father tells Georgie. Georgie snorts with laughter. "It's not a cymbal!" says my brother.

Pappa talks about God being Rebecca's and Sam's shelter. About the prayer shawl also being a symbol of the groom's soul. That Sam is offering his soul to give to my sister. And Georgie wants to know what that word means. "Soul,"
repeats Georgie, but it's more blown that spoken, around the fingers in his mouth. And we're all laughing.

And I'm thinking, Sam is offering his soul? The law is one thing, a soul is another! That's what I'm thinking as my father touches Georgie's chest over his heart, telling him he thinks it must live there. *Sam is giving his soul to my sister, Rebecca*, is all that fills my mind. Sam!

We practice walking between the booths to the canopy. Mamma still isn't dressed. She's cleaning the hall closet. She sends me to the attic with a carton of books to make room for coats. I sit down on a pile of featherbeds and imagine what it will be like to have a bedroom of my own, when something crackles. A brown paper package is pressed between the mattresses. I open a corner and see white lace.

People are arriving. I can hear the bells jingling on the restaurant door. "Maazel Tov!" Uncle Philip is telling Pappa.

"Ruthie!" Mamma calls. "I need you!"

"Mamma!" I'm calling down the stairs. My mother looks up at me. I'm holding up the brown paper package. Mamma's eyes narrow. Then I'm pulling out the end of the French lace veil. My mother starts up the steps.

I'm breathless. "It was between the feather mattresses!" I tell her.

"My God, Ruthie! You found it!" She tears open the paper and holds the veil to her face. "I remember now," says my mother. "I was afraid to use the iron! I washed it and put it there to press! It was there all this

205

time—imagine, right through the move!" Mamma starts to cry. She hugs me, the package crackling between us.

"Mamma, it's a good omen!" I'm saying. My mother has stepped back. She's drying her eyes with the hem of her house dress. "Yes!" she's saying, and she's hugging me again. Then she puts her hand over her mouth. "God heard my prayer!"

"Miriam!" Pappa calls up the steps. "My God," says Mamma. "I've got to get dressed!" The bells on the door are jingling. "Ruthie, help your father!" says my mother, hurrying downstairs, cradling the brown package.

Uncle Phil and Aunt Ida have brought the wedding cake. Pappa's aunt from the Bronx arrives. Then a crowd of Sam's cousins. Cousins Gertie and Sol and the twins arrive. And Pappa's friend Dan, with his camera. The Rabbi comes in with Aunt Flossie. Then a string of Rebecca's friends and a few of Sam's. Aunt Flossie sits down at Aunt Rose's piano. Georgie is holding an empty ring cushion.

"Georgie?" Pappa is asking. Georgie goes upstairs. Then he starts shouting, "Stink! Stink!" It's the worst word Georgie knows.

"Georgie!" Pappa calls up the stairs. Georgie's head appears at the door of his room. "Freddie!" shouts Georgie. Sam's little cousin, Freddie, is squirming down into his chair. Pappa looks over at him. So do I. So does his mother. Then Georgie is standing at the top of the stairs, greens hanging from his cufflinks. He holds up Rebecca's wedding ring for my father to see. "He put it into the fish tank!" complains Georgie.

Freddie's head is down. But Pappa has turned. My mother is hurrying downstairs, her midnight green velvet gown murmuring around her. My grandmother begins down the aisle with Mamma.

Then my sister is standing at the top of the stairs. She's wearing the veil. She's holding a bouquet of white roses. Aunt Flossie starts playing. "Mendelsohn," Aunt Loolie whispers. And I know she's thinking of my Aunt Rose. I imagine her sitting there, where Aunt Flossie is, playing The Wedding March. Rebecca is floating down the stairs like a dream. The queen of France couldn't have been more beautiful.

Tears sting my eyes. Pappa meets Rebecca and they walk down the aisle. Leon steps forward to carry her veil. When my sister stops at the canopy—the hupah—my grandmother raises her head. Rebecca lowers hers. Then Grandma Anna kisses my sister. She touches the veil she carried across the ocean, then wipes her eyes with her big, blunt fingers. Then comes Georgie with the ring cushion. I'm last, scattering violets on the linoleum restaurant floor.

Underneath his prayer shawl Sam waits. His collar fits. He doesn't look so skinny. His smile reminds me of Pappa. Rebecca looks over at him. Through the veil her face seems different. She looks like my sister, but she also seems grown up.

The rabbi is talking about marriage and family. I look at each of my brothers. Georgie is about to put his fingers into his mouth, Mamma is reaching to take his hand. Leon looks like he's about to sneeze. I know one thing: he's forgotten about his football game. He's watching Sam, our brother-in-law, lift the veil from Rebecca's face, the veil that must be a hundred years old, that married women in the family whose names I still don't know. Who in their right mind would want to be at a football game at a time like this?

Then Sam steps on the wine glass, wrapped in a linen

napkin. The sound of its crunch is dull. Suddenly, a droplet of red wine strikes my left eye. It is so odd that I don't tell anyone about it, not until now, here, in this story about my family. But as I write these words it seems to me that drop of wine is about our connection, all of us. My parents, and my grandparents, and my great grandparents, and Aunt Rose, and all the others, people I never met. And it's about Sam and Rebecca, and the way I'm now a little bit married to Sam too. And I'm thinking maybe that's what my mother meant when she said that it was good for our family.

"In the midst of joy there is sorrow!" the Rabbi is saying. "In the midst of sorrow there is joy!" He's telling us the meaning of the broken wine glass.

And just then Aunt Loolie leans over to me and whispers, "Ruthie, this is life!"

Late in the afternoon, Sam and Rebecca run through a shower of rice to Sam's black Oldsmobile. Sam is holding the door open for Rebecca. He kisses me on the cheek. Then he laughs, the way he laughed when I imagined him splashing water at the beach. I kiss him back. He unpins the white carnation from his lapel and pins it into my hair. I just stand there smiling at him. Rebecca and I hug each other. "How would I have gotten married without the veil?" she asks. "I'll come to the beach with you," I answer. When everyone has gone home, my parents are talking at the table about the way the veil turned up. I'm playing with Hannah. Georgie has fallen asleep in his clothes. Leon is doing his homework. When I come to the kitchen to say good night, my parents aren't at the table. I peer through the door to the restaurant. I turn to go upstairs to my room. But not before I see how handsome Pappa is in his dark gray suit, and the way Mamma's midnight green velvet gown brushes against the linoleum as my parents dance.

CPSIA information can be obtained
at www.ICGtesting.com
Printed in the USA
FFHW01n1500101018
48756561-52831FF